Robert Miljan
The Disconnect
Novella

First Chapter

In the current stage of the evolution of humankind, a new beginning is in the coming. A dimension and plane once hidden in the periphery of our planet, veiled by the shadow of hubris, far concealed from human sight, makes itself manifest to those who seek the light. Disabled become those deceptive devices that through invisible frequencies us far and wide connect. The time has come to reacquaint with lost pleasures, puzzles and wonders of old. Find the right moment, the place and the time, taste the sweet words of life's song sublime. Read them aloud, decipher their rhyme, unravel the secrets of infinite time. Read the story in summer's light, read it when the mood is right. Read it in winter's murky dark to saddened tone and spirit hark. No dragons, no kings abound in this story, no battles or telling of some brave knight's glory, – just a celebration of words; one sweet, sad song of where it all went asunder. From the rubble of old a new language is born, a new system devised, erupted of ashes and thunder. The story of one is the story of all and the only pure words are the words of youth, they can't be ignored, they speak the truth.

The same vision opened itself up to Lucas in his sleep on this particularly cold and gray autumn night. In deep, distant sleep immersed, he saw; saw a wonderful cityscape, a cavalry of colossal glass towers, – marvelous monuments scraping the sky up high. Perched up on the highest point, he surveyed through glossy windows an atomic stream of shooting stars, the red rear lights of blazing steel cars, moving, synthesized, harmonized and diffused in an intricate web of bright signs and long traffic lines. He saw silver bullets with shiny white panes piercing the stars; saw hieratic symbols; thin, synthetic screens screaming shiny glitter and perfect bright light; observed organic form structured, simulated, reflected from merchant windows onto the cold gray pavement. He saw the frenetic movement of microscopic figures, scurrying, constantly worrying human beings rushing to inevitable destinations. Urgency and contingency! – The singing songs of nature distorted, muted, concealed behind and diffused throughout a sea of specters and supersonic sound waves.

It's not right with the world, thought Lucas as he awoke from this most disturbing and unnerving of visions. The true ways of the world revealed themselves to him now once more, – a world governed by machines, techno-gadgets, linear forms marching, moving in mechanical rhythm, an atomized organization and circuitry, a self-contained kinetic composition of plastic, fragmentary forms, the reproductive organism transformed into feverish, frenetic stimuli and compensatory thrills. Bright, artificial lights replaced the natural light of the Sun, facilitated and necessitated the constant, unhalting motion of mechanized work. Autonomous dissociation lamed the soul in these times. Lifeless, bloodless, rigid and ritualized repetition and artificial replication severed the cerebral life-cord of humankind, created deadly disinterest, indifference and dumbing distraction. A mistake! It was all one ghastly, misbegotten mistake. This is not how it was supposed to be. Erase it. Rewind. Delete and destroy. Take back it all from whence it came! proclaimed he. But it is real. Lucas closed his eyes, wishing with all his might that he could, for even the briefest moment, forget the current state of things, forget the peculiar string of events that had brought him, brought the sacred force of nature to submission, brought man too far from that natural order of things that governs all of life creation on this insignificant planet. He opened his eyes again and saw with disappointment anew that it was all too real, lowered and shook his head now in foundering recognition of the sheer impossibility and fatal inescapability of it all. Sweet stars! What life, what world is this? thought he. What voice will speak out against the System? What hand will move to action to affect the change that is so much needed? What soul will sound the sirens of distress, will speak of how it all went amiss? Praise be to him who in the time before the fall will stand with unwavering resolve fast to his convictions, will not cower in the face of those dark clouds and thunder that battle against life's eternal bliss wage.

And quickly, all too quickly, it crept. They saw it coming, had been duly forewarned. But those on this planet that great unbending power yielded, with beautiful pictures the masses spellbound held. And dazed, distracted, stupefied, the unmindful, unseeing blissful followed. And not one, or two, or three, not a thousand, not a million could move the unmovable, penetrate the impenetrable, – that infinitely complex and intricate network of partition and treaty that they in titanium forged. The harder one fought, the higher the wall. And so, history had clearly shown that the change that was so much needed could not be exacted by the human hand alone, but that it necessitated the intercession of some greater, more beneficent force far beyond the scope and reach of man.

Love is dead on planet Earth. Currency is love in the time of moving machines. Words have become commodity; prose turned percentage and profit; thought turned property. Nothing more can develop. No voice for those on whom the false light of fame does not shine, for those with whom the weight of material wealth does not lie. Far and ever more distant grew that binding force that connected all things living. How could it be that a race whose source in nature consisted could develop such abhorrence to its own kind, to nature? Then came the great disconnect, that disproportionate imbalance and sickened state of the system that dissymmetry in the hearts of so many incited and the lines of the frequency between man and nature severed. Abandoned became the striving for the good of the whole. And there could be no peace, no freedom as long as so much as even one suffered. He saw compassion supplanted by conspiring utility, opportunism and exploit. Entangled in a complex system, a network of countless and trivial worries and troubles bred a thousand more, each one greater than the former. Like plague they grew. Fruitless indifference bred obsequious complacency. The cold, surgical objectivity by which man was from all sides surrounded necessitated from him unceasing participation, assimilation, blind complicity. Alienated, disarmed and disengaged by his own helplessness; impotent and paralyzed in the face of insurmountable walls, he found himself inclined to construct always new clever, cunning, crafty and calculating methods of distraction, ever new mechanisms to cope, to justify, to rationalize the wretched state of the world and the constraining injunctions of administration. He realized that life in the system could only be endured in distraction and that the life one lives is tolerable only in complicity, obedience, submission, – in the ebb and flow, and not in the clashing waves of a tide that beats violently against the jagged rocks of dividing walls. Revolution: a forbidden and exiled notion, – inconceivable, unweighed. Where did they go wrong? How could one even begin to rationalize, to truly fathom the progression of a state of being so

10

starkly, so inconceivably opposed to the natural state of the universe that had implanted its seed in man in the very beginning of the dawning of his primal intellect? Was it man's desire to at last free himself of his human lot that had made him so vulnerable, so utterly prepared to embrace the false-conceived notion of deliverance or salvation at the hand of the machine, of a system that promised progress; progress that never came?

Artificial intelligence could never replace the conceptual cord connecting all life, which perpetuates itself in the gift of procreation. It lacked most of all the human element of love. It represented much more than a haunting dream; it was a pestilent disease that probed and infected the nervous system of all life creation; it seized the body, the mind, the soul; it devoured the entire whole. The rotten comprise the whole and the ones who resist the chemical flow represent the abnormality, the inconsistency. And the destruction, the pain, the fear, the pollution saw no end. They called this progress, – a natural step in the evolution of mankind. But Lucas, along with a select few of the illuminated ones, saw it for what it was: a lie, a beautiful, hideous, aesthetic lie;

had come to the at once emancipating and incarcerating realization that it was indeed of little merit to be adjusted to a profoundly corrupt system; saw that there was indeed scarcely any virtue in a life unquestioned, a life unchallenged; came to the at once nourishing and damning conclusion that a life unexamined is a life hardly worth living. All that remain on this planet now are but a few sparse particles of the essence of life's source never ending. For the sake of this source, – and for its sake alone –, those celestial beings saw this planet worth saving. And of the last threads of the essence eternal, a small but significant grain of which still lived on in us, they wove their new design, brought to reconvene the forms of their own world in ours, for the forms of old sufficed no more; the system simply ceased to work, could no longer hold.

He stomped and roared; trembled and convulsed in the face of human struggle and human indifference and wondered if man were at all ever suited for an existence apart from the striving toward the fulfillment of primal physical drives, passions and instincts. In the university lecture hall, he and a handful of students, – relatively younger than he –, observed intently a philosophical lecture on the subject of the origin of species. And he began to daydream. Soaking in the pleasant warmth of the light of the Sun that shone on him through the window, he contemplated the purpose of the potential advantage, – or disadvantage –, in the evolutionary sense, of the faculties of emotion and memory, of our capacity to reason, reflection and circumspection. What advantages, if any, did creatures of the animal kingdom, for instance, stand to profit from the absence thereof? The proponents of enlightenment and reason are quick to pronounce their judgment of the unforgiving cruelties and arbitrary indifferences of nature that are common and most pronounced among those to whom we refer as the baser forms of life of this planet, would but defend this same struggle among humans that they in these lowly creatures find so abhorrent. There was, when it came down to it, no fundamental difference between our species, really, thought Lucas. It was, in the end, still basic primitive passion that moved us, the brutal, carnal struggle for survival concealed behind the veil of contrived culture and civilization. Free enterprise they called it. Hypocrisy in hyperbole! The mechanism of survival was still there; man had progressed only to more refined; infinitely more clever and meticulous methods of dominance over his own. Men killed with contract and currency; written documents and decrees; clauses and stipulations were the refined weapons of the system in these times when diamonds and gold and green dollar bills became the gleaming stars in our eyes. And what disharmony can one find in the kingdom of those to whom we refer as the beasts of the jungle that we cannot find in our own world? There is a heightened malevolence in the notion of a species that possesses the singular gift of reason, but that chooses instead to take it for granted. There exists, furthermore, a naïve innocence in the way of being of those of the animal kingdom, at the sight of which man shows a secret, desperate, longing reverence and cause to shame, – shame, for they remind him of his infinite removal from such a state, from a simpler way of life that he had once enjoyed long, long ago, but that he had long lost and forgotten.

Lucas thought how foolish it was of the human race to have clung to the naïve notion that they would be there throughout the endless years. He remembered the story of a message that had years ago been transmitted into the skies above; a series of frequencies, of binary symbols that carried the imprint of our genetic code in the hopes that if there were intelligent life forms out there, they would respond. It was only later in life that he could see the grave arrogance in our belief that intelligence could be measured according to our own principles. What other reference point do we have than our own miniscule presence in the midst of endless stars, this limited sphere that still remains the beginning and the end of our consideration? Were a species from somewhere far out there to visit us, it would naturally follow that they would be superior to us in ways unfathomable. Would they receive us as but primitives? He thought once more of the ideas contained in every single book he had read throughout the span of his entire life, of all that had been transmitted to him until this point; thought then of greed and war; thought how infinitely far removed we are from the one, the only true supreme intellect. One just had to look up into the stars on a clear night to understand the true verity of this idea, the idea, namely, that the castles we have built in the name of that which we call progress are rendered meaningless obsolescence when one considers the illimitable luminescence and exceeding significance of the true light. Perhaps that is why so many of us seldom look up into the night sky; it frightens us, leaves us trembling in fear, reminds us of our insignificance in the boundlessly greater scheme of things. The realization of the sheer enormity of it all terrifies us beyond measure, might even lay cause for us to question our undying and unwavering compliance to the system we have created on this planet, a system that is so far removed from that which one could ever have envisioned. He looked deeper then, thought of the state in which our primitive ancestors must have lived hundreds of thousands, yes, even millions of years ago, and wondered if the human race were not somehow inevitably drawn to a life of distraction and self destruction. He weighed the thought that the purpose of life; the answer to the perplexing riddle of our existence was perhaps not to be found in the self-conceived notion of some profound striving toward progress and perfection of spirit and intellect, but in the mere existing for the sake of existing; wondered if there were any other reality than human strife and struggle. Was nature an unforgiving tyrant? Will not the Sun, which

16

gives us life, one day, too, extinguish her precious light?

Shame on him whose eyes cannot see! Had he the power, would he with the merciless might of all his fighting fury and in the name of all that is harmonious and just, call to stand trial those who had instrumented such abominable atrocities against creation. On the count of grave indifference and haughty, insolent pride, he would condemn them to finity, – the most feared of all fates, that punishment that withholds from man admittance to the realm of the infinite. Sweet the fate of the elucidated among them and rightly so spared would judgment of those be who had suffered so much in the dubious times of the great disconnect, when the world we know had become far and farthest removed from the radiant light of the supreme source, the spark of which so many beautiful, hopeless, forsaken fates fueled. They who held the preponderance of capital in their hands; they who dared to place themselves in league with the same precious stars to which all life owes its existence; they who led us to falsely and foolishly believe that scarcity could exist on a planet teeming with such abundant profusion; yes, they who every last ray of bright life-light from the planet plundered, – they would be the first to pay. Vile blasphemy! And how they would pay; they would pay greatly and dearly. For them, those fascinating forms from celestial spheres descended would spare no mercy. And down they came from the violet skies to save the day, to renounce man of his tyrannical dominion over this planet, to tear from his selfish hand that prodigal gift that to him only wretched exploit and excess became.

He had the indelible and undeniable privilege of having spent the prime of his life, his youth, in precisely that so very brief and singular period before humanity's pinnacle ascension in all the facets of scientific and technological advancement. One much younger in years had once asked him: "What did they do in the time before those devices?" to which he, with a half smile, a glint of joy in his eyes and a tone of exuberant pride replied: "We talked, we wondered, we read; we wrote secret notes, songs and hand-written letters; we met in parks, by the entrance of train stations, at bus stops; we walked on train tracks at sunset, climbed trees, explored and were tickled with joy when the world revealed to us some new and hidden wonder." In the few invaluable and critical years that marked the heights of our civilization, preceding ideologies, ideas and philosophies had exceptionally converged, concretized and culminated in an impossible and beautiful conundrum. But progress came at a weighty price. Cogs, wheels, steam engines and pressing machines propelled the rapid progress; drones of workers marched in conform and regulatory routine to carry on feeble back the burden of lofty progress. We reaped the selfish rewards of the labor that they with hungry wombs; boiled and blistered fingers suffered and on broken back carried.

And on the cusp of that sensational ascension, man had neared a revolutionary discovery; had devoted excruciating effort to the search for a curious substance, – a subatomic particle, the main ingredient in an entity they classified as dark matter. Perhaps it was no coincidence that those creatures intervened precisely at the point at which man had been on the verge of locating this particle that would have forever and irrevocably changed everything. Perhaps it was because they knew, knew what devastating potential that such a discovery would have had were it to have fallen in the hands of man. And they would have been

19

justified in their conjecture, for any significant advancement or discovery, man had transformed into weapon, – a mere further means through which to exact power and tyranny over his own and destruction over the planet. There was indeed infinitely more to the outer regions of the space that we inhabit than met the eye. It was perhaps in the space of that matter; in that fold, that crease in time continuum, invisible to the human eye and undetectable by any human instrument of visual detection, for that matter, in which these beings resided. Mastery or manipulation of this matter by the hand of man would have cataclysmically compromised their existence. So, in the interest of their own survival and in the name of the mission on which they were soon to embark, they saw it only pertinent, no, were unduly provoked and pressed to make their presence known.

It was out of much more than mere nostalgic sentimentality or virtue of coincidence of his youthful prime in these times to which Lucas could assert such claims of progress; it was rather trifling factuality, in fact. Not only he, who from childhood on possessed a rather unusually keen insight into the world, but the general consensus of the masses was that this generation had experienced an unfathomable and unprecedented acceleration in the advancement of scientific discovery. These were exciting times indeed, and although the system that they had built up in industry resulted in the natural resurgence of unnatural and unarguably negative implications, among the most fatal of which was the exhaustion of the Sun's light and Earth's precious resources, they bore nonetheless the stamp of unparalleled dynamism and hope. They were there to be reaped by a few, in a short and remarkably finite span of time. After all, what was fear of the Sun's dying light and the destruction of Mother Nature compared to such thrilling wonders; in the face of all those plastic toys and plastic joys; the moving pictures; the gleaming, glittering lights and hopes of counterfeit heights? Were one to turn off the lights, however, one would see with glaring clarity, the pretty lie in all its gruesome, naked horror. Exiting times indeed!

But what good are shiny treasures and empty pleasures in a world that longs no more the human touch? Old sacred traditions have lost their meaning; seasons' greetings are now but empty words. Ritual candles continue to burn long after human beings have lost the will to strive, to yearn. Written contracts and invisible walls prevent the yearning soul to roam his natural domain, his earthly home. Divided they create distinctions and assert dominance over their own. Hand written books, philosophies and ideas are getting old; a disenchanted generation is growing cold; honor and admiration dying for those who age and wisdom hold. What legacy will they leave behind when numbers and figures threaten to enfetter the soul, enfeeble the mind?

Second Chapter

He was the product of a budding union between a stern and morose but loving mother and a jovial father of a most pleasing disposition. Nature, arbitrary in her ways, however, had bestowed upon this particular one a preponderance of the more submissive and softer sensibilities of the feminine race. It was perhaps this partial predilection, to most, an intolerable aberration, to which one could attribute his gentle, feeling soul. It was perhaps even uncertain as to whether biological or social circumstances, or a combination of the two, were at play in the forming of this inimitable child, this singular product of unrivaled circumstance. He was living proof that behind each single life lies an intricate blueprint and that a myriad of conditions must exist in order that a certain product come into being. It was a felicitous fluke of fate that mother and father had scarcely imposed restraint on the flourishing of his natural gifts and sentimental temperament. It can even be said that they exhibited an indifference, yes, an even subtle disinterest in any and all things pertaining to the mental, emotional and spiritual conditions of his dawning youth, such that he had been left to his own devices to mold himself to his own convention. It can be said of him that he, in these remarkably critical and impressionable years, developed an uncanny consciousness and awareness of the apparent shortcomings of mother and father, of his peers, of his mentors, of humankind. He discovered the pain that comes from having altogether surpassed one's parents, yes, even one's mentors in mental and emotional intelligence.

He contemplated anything and everything, left not one stone unturned; reflected often on the dichotomy of body and soul and, in some instances, even on the precise point at which the soul enters the physical body, and whether, in certain unfathomable circumstances, the soul had in fact failed to infuse itself into the physical form of some, leaving, as a result, a soulless body. And the more he probed this matter, the more he could find justification for his belief that there existed in this world people who seemed to have been devoid of that which one could discern as a soul, – if there were at all such a thing. This led him inevitably to the question: Was this willed by some greater force? Or was it perhaps a mere unfortunate cosmic coincidence, a serendipitous snag, a flaw in the knotty thread of things, in the convoluted link of cause and effect? Or had it been taken from him? For Lucas, the latter seemed the most plausible, given the wretched, decaying state of the world. He, more than any other, could attest to the notion that life in the current system was indeed a full-out war for the preservation of the soul, and he could find no greater irony than in the idea that those in whose hands the gavel of justice lie were the very same ones who had most significantly contributed to the deterioration of the system and the destruction of planet Earth.

Left to his own devices, Lucas had taught himself at an unusually unripe age and by means of some strange and mysterious method of inference, the tools of self-reflection, introspection and deep insight into his surroundings, into the atrocious injustices of a corrupt system, yes, into the black-holed abyss of life. He read between the lines, nourished and cultivated the seed of creativity where the parental and institutional hand had failed. Not that they had been grossly inadequate in the fulfillment of their instructive duties or commitments in any fundamental way, but their circumstances, their own genesis had reduced them to the basic needs of necessity, practicality and subsistence, to concerns of the physical here and now. An unusually early union of mother and father had allowed for the absence of a disparity in years between parent and child that is typical in most families, and which naturally establishes a discontinuity between the generations. Scarcely having entered into the age when most are still transitioning into the early stages of the pragmatic life, they had already, and all too early, learned to know the pains of ripe and stern adulthood, had already produced two children and taken on the burdens that only those typically more advanced in years learn to know. Fortunately, and in spite of this, he, unforeseeably and inexplicably, suffered no significant delays in his intellectual and spiritual evolution. In fact, these conditions only served to amplify and accelerate the cultivation of the light in him. His parents were migrants from the land of such Slavic muses as Svarog and Dazdbog. New settlers in this land in which their children had been born, they were preoccupied with the struggles of acclimatization, integration and assimilation in this land that was still very new and strange to them. But Lucas stood to reap great profit from this union. It endowed him exposure to a dynamic and multiplicitous array of experience. The acquisition from infancy and onwards of a second language, of a second history, – the product of the union of two diverging and colliding cultures and opposing sensibilities, only increased his skills in the sphere of perception and intuition; served to emancipate him from the hemming homogeneity of his homeland. Most of all, he developed a supra-human capacity for empathy, learned to the very core and at a heavy cost how fragile the flesh and sensitive the soul in the face of obstacles.

A lack of affection in the familiar sphere was not of any impeding consequence for Lucas. If anything, he had been loved too much, at least as concerns physical wellbeing. This made a lasting impression on him, would however, in his later years, manifest itself in an inability to ever completely stand on his own two feet. Recognizing the improbability of the potential for true growth were he to have continued his existence in this stifling place of his childhood, he imposed on himself a self-willed detachment from the home; made the trenching but nonetheless necessary decision to leave. The new independence that ensued manifested itself consequently in a destructive and all-consuming excess of will and self-indulgence; brought him to a full-pledged rebellion against the arbitrary inequity of life, against those who had dared to judge his placid soul. And after several years of rash decision and impulsive behavior, it finally neutralized, leaving him not unscathed by the passions and risky explorations of these years.

And, when it was all over, this phase that had accounted for a considerable chapter of his adolescent life seemed to him, in retrospect, like nothing more than a mere fleeting dream, an indistinguishable, vaporous mist of blended memory and experience in the greater and infinitely more significant scheme of things. Only familiar melodies would bring him back to particular moments of this time. But, as in anything, experience and memory, from which music had namely borrowed its inspiration, occupy two disparately opposing poles, the destructive and constructive, the degenerative and regenerative. He, perhaps more than anyone, wished that he could expel, yes, altogether exile the least pleasurable of these memories into forgetting oblivion, was however not fully unaware of the great necessity of even these in forming the peculiar person he had become. Perplexing paradox! Only our inherent mechanism of repression prevents these memories from ever completely consuming and destroying us, and he wished, more than anyone, that the state in which we would find ourselves after this life, – if there did at all exist such a thing –, would be one in which only the positive, happy and life-affirming impulses and memories persist. But, like the composition of all that which surrounds us, of a universe in which both positive and negative ions and protons constantly collide, and the consideration that all the matter of the universe, and, yes, even we, are composed of the sweet stuff of stars, made the existence of both positive and negative memories and emotions an irrefutable inevitability. The ideal state, he often thought, would be one in which we were freed from all memory of our previous life altogether. He was a firm believer in a dictum he had once read in a philosophy book, which professed that the first step to true understanding of the world, of life, is wishing never to have been born at all. But, we are alive! He saw at once a simple verity and complex contradiction in the notion of conceiving of the potentiality of not having existed at all, for the very conception that allowed for the consideration of such a possibility necessitated existence, or rather, was facilitated by mere virtue of existence, and not ever having existed negates the very possibility of the state in which we are very much alive, for if we were not to have existed, how would we possibly be able to conceive of a state in which we could negate the very life that does not exist? For we cannot possibly conceive of a state in which we are not conceiving. The notion of the cessation of such a state, of a conceiving mind conceiving of its existence before or after its own existence, seemed the most absurd of absurdities, evoked only incalculably further questions, created an impossible philosophical dilemma. These were the types of questions with which he occupied himself. They consumed him, – more than they had the right to –, and he recognized that they had prevented him from truly living and from tasting the sweet nectar of life.

He had been grossly maladjusted to the realities of ruthless competition and struggle for self-preservation; fully and utterly unprepared for all the tests, the taunting, the teasing; terribly ill equipped for the grueling realities that awaited; learned all too early the dying agony of humiliation, while his peers, who seemed somehow to have been preconditioned and bred for such hardships, wandered effortlessly and unscathed through life. Sticks and stones, they broke his bones, but names, – they always hurt him. This life came but once, and they; they deprived him of its joys; robbed of him his youth. And for this, there was no recompense, no reparation. He remembered the first initiation, – the first sorrowful walk to school, the deep anxiety of abandonment that trampled his crying soul, his sweeping sensitivity. The cruel realities he had endured in these years were, however, of crucial and critical importance to his evolution, for they evoked and inspired in him thoughtful reflection; careful, scrutinizing introspection and startling insight into the deepest, darkest shadows of our existence.

No, he was special, one of a kind, a gem for his years. Emotion was intelligence, and this particular boy was, beyond a shadow of a doubt, emotional, intelligent; possessed the rare and remarkable power of keen insight and perception into the world. All of these preconditions and predispositions left him isolated and secluded in these unripe years from the outer spheres of social contracts and pacts of his peers. It is predominately this self-imposed solitude that gave him the strength he needed in later years to face the existential problems confronting him, confronting all of mankind. Although these qualities left him thoroughly unsuitable and unequipped for the transition into the world that awaited him, as regards all those trivial pragmatics and practicalities, they did something more profound; they made him more privy to see, to truly see into the nature of things, to read between the lines. A dangerous gift indeed! – Dangerous because it allowed him to see behind the surface of things, to see the true ways of the world. It was no surprise then that he found himself gravely inapt for and grossly discontented and dissatisfied with the shallow surface of things.

It was not long until he discovered the tantalizing wonders hidden behind words; they revealed to him worlds and fates unattainable, experiences unimaginable. At an age when most children content themselves with trivial games and simple musings, he had already begun deciphering the meaning behind metaphors, symbols and sweet soliloquies in books; found in their hyperboles, juxtapositions and similes, a common ground, a parallel for his own experience. The plights of philosophers, of poets, of men in stories became his own; he found them inexorable, inextricable from his own struggles and fate. They fulfilled him immeasurably, forged in him the force of keen wisdom and true knowledge of the world that reveals itself to those who seek and demand of life its sweet and sour secrets. Unsatisfied with the limiting limitations of his limited sphere, he saw a million other potentialities and possibilities; a myriad of innumerable fates and destinies unraveled before him, and this he could not accept, for he saw at once that they were unattainable. But his existence became more fulfilled, deeper and richer for it for the dreams and hopes that they in him invigorated. While the cynical world called him a hopeless dreamer, those like him were the only true realists, for they saw the world as it really was.

And from his sorrow emerged the most beautiful story. Had he found himself in any other circumstance; had he not had the sustaining force of words to hold him up and guide him through it all; had he found any slight divergence from the life he had known, things would have been very different for him. He recognized his great fortune. Fate would not see him fall, would hold him up on shaky ground to see him bring to fruition the duty that his entire life in sleep awaited and its divine purpose would soon reveal. He was an artist. And was it not the divine duty of the artist to instruct man on matters of the metaphysical, the transcendental; to allegorize the pains, sorrows and misery of man's existence in a way that was most comprehensible to him? Could it be that he belonged to those chosen few, to that legacy of philosophers, poets and authors, – those critical thinkers and theorists who criticized, protested and disseminated the injustices of the system in which they lived? The notion had long become apparent to Lucas that there existed indeed an undeniable and inexorable parallel between his own fate and the decaying state of the world. And he was uncertain as to whether his view of the world was a product of his own flawed perspective, his distorted way of seeing things. Was the world really so? Or was it just a manifestation of his gross sensitivity, the symptom of an inherently defective world?

He harbored an insatiable thirst for language, amassed very early an extensive and ever-growing archive of words and phrases. And, when his native tongue ceased to stimulate, he found further rousing in a foreign language or two, which he mastered swiftly and well. Words are a peculiar thing; like music, they have the curious power to penetrate, through means of the outer senses, the inner realm of the soul. But just as music encompasses the harmony of form and content; metric rhythm and melody, so too is a beautiful literary work the delicate balance of abstract symbolism and formalistic structure. Like the notes of a tantalizing musical masterpiece, the full beauty and artistic potential of a literary text lends itself not only to a precise and structured alignment and ordering of the words it contains, but to an intangible essence. It is a difficult undertaking to transform thoughts into eloquent words. If one were to remove the perceiving mind from the equation, words would be nothing more than but mere meaningless, indecipherable symbols.

Thoughts and ideas are highly abstract entities. Countless impulses evade us. A story, like music, is the ethereal balance between form and content; a composition of words turned magical metaphor. The ideal story is one that is at once all thought and thought become wonderful word, constraint and unrestrained license; the most subtle intercourse and interplay of musical lyric and melody occupying the middle realm of reality and illusion, dream and our waking state. A beautiful story is one that reads like the effortless flow; the crossing back and forth, to and fro of these two otherwise antonymous and seemingly incompatible spheres, so that, upon reading and reciting the written words, we are rendered fully oblivious to this interplay, to the effect that we almost forget the source from which they sprung. One word evokes endless associations and allusions. We lose ourselves in the words; concepts and ideas detach themselves from the symbols that hold them and take on a life of their own. The image transcends static, constraining form, sprouts wings and thus becomes eternalized. Lucas shared a deep and profound appreciation and understanding of the importance of all of these elements in writing, in language, in art, and years of devotion to language had granted him a humble acknowledgement of the unworldly nature and symbolic potential of words.

He found his highest creative inspiration and solace in the silent night when the lights went off. The dim, tangerine light of the bedside lamp mimicked that of the setting Sun sensationally; it glazed his mellow soul; warmed and subdued the worried wonders of the day. He found a haven, – a sweet disconnect in the hours during which the weary world lie in unconscious oblivion, when the absence of the static frequencies of frenetically moving shapes and forms, the cosmopolitan clings and clangs that during the waking hours served to diffuse his thoughts; confuse his thinking mind, his feeling soul, were temporarily, in the lulling silence of the night, put to rest. Oh, how he suffered the strains and pains of each day, abhorred so much the sight and sound of stirring people. The hours of the day carried the urgent, impatient hopes of the imminent night, and the night a futile delay and denial of the inevitable tomorrow, – always tomorrow that with it brought new pain and sorrow.

He was reminded of his frequent visits to the school library where he would often lose himself in a labyrinth, a cavalry of towering bookshelves. In the cozy crevices and corners that they provided, he would find solace from the frightening world; would skim manically endless titles upon titles and random excerpts; felt a tantalizing delight in the thought that he, and he alone, had discovered a hidden gem among the uniform rows upon rows of inconspicuous books that had been previously, so he presumed, undiscovered and unread by any other soul. If one were to compile every single book ever written, every periodical ever printed, every play, every diary, every piece of paper onto which a thought, a precious piece of prose or a secret note were written, how high would they reach? he often wondered. He would take in the sweet scent of the suffocated books that had been franticly perused during the thick of the school year only to be completely abandoned in the summer months after the students had left and the inclination to read had declined. The experience was for him one that engaged all of the senses; was as much a tactual and auditory experience as it was a visual one. He took great delight in the sound of the words as he enunciated them aloud to himself. He loved the texture of the surface of hard cover books, much preferred them to soft covers; coarse, matte and slightly yellow or brown tinted pages to crisp, fresh and new glossy white paper for the air of old wisdom that they emanated. What excited, slightly frightened and baffled him was the notion of the sheer immutability of the words found in the books, or rather, of the ideas that they embodied. They were there forever, firmly rooted, all enduring, – or so he would have liked to believe. Yet, they seemed to have taken on a new meaning with each new inspection, opened themselves up to numberless interpretations. Would they cease to exist once man was extinguished from this planet? No, they are eternal! They are the vessel, he thought; the capturing of an intangible essence forged of and sprung from something so seemingly effortless as a thought, a feeling, and that power, that incommensurably intricate faculty in us that thought, emotion and intent sparks and into words transmits; that power, that force is the transmission of an essence, an output of some magical energy that in us resides.

Third Chapter

He muddled in misty, autumn-toned array along cobblestone paths cloaked in leaves of bright orange, copper and red toward a marvelous building built in old gothic style and adorned with stunning green vines of ivy that still eagerly climbed the old stone fortress of knowledge and covered almost the entire exterior, leaving only sparse openings that revealed small patches of old withered gray stone. It impressed unto one at once an air of old wisdom, pretense and material prosperity, which extended not only to the architectural landscape of the collegiate grounds, but to all that which surrounded it, from the pretentious automobiles parked in pristine precision along the bright, fluorescent-green moss covered stones of the campus to the carefully orchestrated and well-rehearsed mimicries of social grace that reverberated through a sea of beige tweed, corduroy and old spice; well rehearsed overtures that emanated from the mouths of perfectly poised figures, each and every one so nondescript and so tragically indistinguishable from the other. It all seemed to coalesce, however, and he could not feign that it did not all, in its own right and in the shadow of the most opportune light, boast some kind of mesmeric magnetism. Rain, cloud and fog complemented this tapestry wonderfully, as if they fit into that mood, that bleak and musty canvas of academia. It was all somehow conducive to leisured recline during lengthy philosophical debates among seasoned scholars on matters of deep intellectual gravity in mahogany chairs in rooms draped in plaid, brown and burgundy over whiskey and rye. With the fall of every leaf, with each growing gust of the fresh, cool and brisk autumn breeze, so too grew his need to finally stamp in words, before winter's bitter, stark cold and dark, the story of his, of humanity's plight. And he was that very last leaf that clung to the tree, that, as it let go, cried out to winter, who in the shadows lurked: "I, Lucas, herewith surrender myself unimpassioned to you." And after months of slumbered repose and resignation, jolted to action to finish the unfinished deed, the words came to him, brushed him like the hand of a dear and loving friend. And so, after all the pain he had endured, utterly trampled and defeated by life, he had once again found his way back to words. And

indeed, the most wonderful words sprang forth from the pages that told of the fallacy of the preceding ages. He filled the holes and empty spaces, a rhyme or two to press the present worry, to give prominence to that pronounced mood that so deeply moved him; rounded out the jagged ends until a peculiar story had come together, in rain, in clouds, in stormy weather.

On his homeward way from the circular head of the long, opulent linden tree-lined promenade, along which he had frequently taken his walks, a group of eight or ten youths in his path stood huddled before the entrance of one of this nation's most prominent and preeminent private academies. Indignantly obstructing the sidewalk, they forced him now into an impossible impasse, into the decision, namely, of weighing the difficult recourse of pushing his way through the huddled mass of irreverent youths or avoiding them altogether by making a sudden and hasty detour onto the traffic-ridden avenue. There was the further alternative of crossing to the other side of the street altogether, but he realized that it was too late, that such a maneuver would have garnered even more unwanted attention from the youths or have made them privy to the insecurity that had triggered such cowardice in him. His objective, when he had found himself in such similar compromising circumstances before, had always been to pass by as inconspicuously as possible. Finding himself now coerced into a confrontation with the insolent juveniles, however, Lucas saw at this moment no other mode of action more viable than to arm himself with a mock cocksureness commensurate to that which the leader of this group had imbued, the same look of disdain toward him that he had reserved for anyone who reminded him of his former oppressors.

What does the animal do when it knows it is trapped, knows it is over, yet calls upon its vital instincts to escape its ineluctable fate, to flee from its predator? Lucas had had in his youth much time to study his oppressors, had compiled a precise profile of the predator, whose characteristics and demeanor, he found, were so unoriginally similar. Without any real effort, he was, by virtue of experience and some deeper instinct in him, now, too, almost immediately, quite effortlessly, intuitively and with great certainty, able to discern among the lot, the leader of the group. Long, blond hair slicked back, draped in lavish and visibly exorbitant attire more suited to an established man more mature in years than a youth of his age, cigarette deliberately poised in one hand, elbow perched on the shoulder of an inferior classmate, recognizing that he had become the object of Lucas' inspection, offended and determined to deflect his timid gaze, returned the other's glance of disdain and produced the shield of battle, feigning all the while cool disregard and devil-may-care. And so, Lucas had on this occasion too suffered, and now, here, survived the encounter that had on him had far weightier a bearing than it should have. He continued on his way, maimed, head down in shame for having allowed himself to be slighted by this incident that by most would likely have gone altogether undignified.

He had long absolved himself of any blame for his heightened sensitivity; saw himself justified in his reasoning, his over-thinking when it came to such circumstances. He paid his dues. They were to blame. It was they who made him so. And how could they, how could the world expect that he be anything else? He, nor they, could negate the conditions that made him so. And how insolent of them to expect that he take on the burden of absolution! Repugnant reality! He walked home, once more deeply affected, despising his state, shaking his head in recognition of this impossible, sticky, hideous reality for which, he felt, there wasn't, or ever would be, any resolve or true restitution for the indignities he had been forced to endure.

He deplored and grew to despise to the core those to whom favoritism, bias and partial preference had been bestowed, especially as regards physical prowess and beauty, naturally because he possessed neither, but more because they were not borne of the type of hardship that had formed him. But such was this damned and deplorable world in which he lived. What twisted, thorned and double-handed trick of fate was this? What gods were they that willed it so? In the same breath, it was indeed a felicitous force that gave those who that outward luster lacked a higher sense with regard to matters of the mind, the heart, the soul. He saw in the persecutory stares of the people he passed on the street the trembling image of his greatest fears and anxieties reflected, cast back at him like a sharp, poisonous arrow. But he broke the burrier of their guarded glances; saw in their eyes small inklings of the secrets that they guarded. And something special, some magic glitter in his eyes seemed to have evoked in the eyes of those who had had the indelible fortune of crossing his path, of entering into his sphere, a reaction of threatening offence. That singular sparkle that some would call a gift from the heavens, they saw as a trespass against and condemnation of the life they led, of the nullifying, stunting and stagnating staleness of their bleak and utterly tragic suburban lives. There is no greater malice than human indifference. Only arrogance and ignorance feign disinterest, nonchalance. Seldom do people issue so much as even a gentle, affirming look of acceptance of the presence of those whom they pass on the street, seldom so much as a simple smile of acknowledgment of the other's equally shared membership in the human race. A simple and effortless gesture of recognition moves mountains.

He deplored furthermore those who kept pets and gardens. Hideous hypocrisy! As detached and as far removed from nature as modern man could be, they fancied themselves to have shared some false-perceived kinship with nature. But he saw it for what it was, namely, a selfish inclination to subjugate, for man loves conditionally;

loves most that over which he can exercise and assert power. Readily and quite effortlessly displaying indifference toward their fellow man, they would spare not the least expense in bestowing the most outrageous of luxuries unto their pets. Similarly, pruning and primming, they impose unto the flowers of their precious fenced-in gardens, much like they do with anything else, a containable and controllable structure onto everything they touch. It fulfills them, gives them the feeling of authority, of satiating supremacy.

And soon came winter. He was walking the way he often went along the path dividing the blocks of lonely suburban boxes in which lonely souls resided. It was quiet; so frighteningly, so disturbingly quiet. Above lie a faint, orange-crested moon, and in the air, the sedating scent of firewood burning evoked the memory of campfire and marshmallows roasting. The snow began to gently fall. And he, shivering in his scanty coat, wishing that he was concealed behind a fortress of feather and wool, suddenly overcome with the most unsettling worry, his legs grew tired and he wished with all his might that he could just fall unheard and unnoticed into the thick bed of soft, pure white powdered snow, to mute the present worry, to fall asleep, never to wake again, to simply wish himself out of existence. He no longer even missed or mourned the light of the Sun, which had an eternity ago forsaken him, left him to waste away in the absence of her comforting warmth. He lingered for a while, as if trying to remember something he had long forgotten, but that force that sets memory in motion momentarily faltered now. The insignificance of it all, however, appeared to him at this very moment with such clarity. He felt so detached, so apart from life, from the trees. He thought, he wished, he hoped; if he were the snowy owl, wide green eyes and feathers white, white as the winter snow, he would sit and bask in moonlight's glow. He would hold dominion over the silent night, would mourn no more the dying light. Rabbits and mice would be his prey; he would hunt at night and sleep by day. Perched on the branch of the highest tree, he would spread his wings for all to see. He would wait and watch in the quiet night, not a stirring soul would escape his sight. The howling wind would be his friend, and the winter night would have no end. And as the snow softly fell and sky and earth fused in a fog of precious and pure, white light, the singularity of life, of his place and presence on this planet became, crisp as the pure, white snow, apparent to him. He realized what great fortune, what singular gift it was to experience each season, each winter anew, and saw that the changing of the seasons remained the only means with which to tell the passage of time. But the constant cycle remains the same; only we change and inevitably perish. And when we're gone, a new set of eyes will behold this very same image of a day very much similar to this, no, in fact, identical to this one in every way.

And so, with the sounds of progress absent, life's lulling silence pierced his soul and he felt and heard the sounds of the barren emptiness of life: Survival. Surviving. Living. Being. Breathing. Silence. Gentle wind. Snow. Cold. Hunger. Shelter. It's real! It's all so real! Suddenly, he found himself in a summer scene immersed, lying down in the midst of a dandelion field and looking up at the stars on a perfectly clear night in a place far removed from the city lights, absent from the stifling sounds of progress, – just he, the cool green grass beneath him and the vast sky above. Dusk, with his crimson cheeks, emerged, illuminating the aurora of astronomical, cosmic clusters, a myriad of constellations of infinitely distant stars, star-crossed skies and fireflies. Lucas lie on the cool grass, gazing into the wide-open spaces, in dazed contemplation of the infinite vastness of it all. Is there life out there? he wondered, as he looked up into the heavens above and wondered how man could not always have been there throughout the endless years, how he could not possibly be part of a pre determined plan, the true idea of creation. Does not the infinite manifest itself in attributes of the finite? thought he. And are all things finite not but a mere extension of the infinite? What did ancient man think when he looked up at the night sky and the stars? Did he shrink each time in fear and amazement anew? He could feel the earth move, actually feel it move! And he defied for a moment the confining force of gravity, ascended, submitted himself to and immersed himself completely in the skies and star-crossed spaces until he lost all point of reference and felt as if he was, – the ground below descending –, floating in oblivion. Submerged in hypnotic space dream, he saw specs of shimmering stardust, heard tantalizing space chimes whispered thousands of light years ago and echoed through the colliding spaces of the vast night. And when he finally came down, when a touch of the cool, green grass and the chirp of a cricket brought him gently back, he felt for a brief spell thereafter disoriented, found his senses shuffled and ruffled about, and, above all, he found himself immeasurably enriched and moved by this brief sojourn in nature and in stars that had brought him the much needed reminder of the sheer insignificance of it all.

And with these rare moments, he stamped into time his mark, as if to proclaim that he, Lucas, the soft and timid wonderer, on this singular summer night, in these rare and precious times before the fall, had rested his heavy head here on this very spot and set his wide, bewildered and bedazzled eyes upon the stars that made him. And they, the stars, would forever bear witness to his existence, would carry the eternal breath of his longing gaze. So little was required to leave one's mark on this planet; no great deed, no profound feat, just but a momentary recognition of life and of one's place within the big, frightening picture of it all. And it is in the inarticulate that we find clarity, – that delicate space between the hard and rough surface of things, between matter and empty space, – the stuff of which poems, stories, songs and sweet lullabies are made. And that which we cannot with our eyes see, with our fingers touch, – therein lie the breath of our design, of things of higher virtue such as true justice, beauty and love. And he thought that heaven must be something like a perpetual sunrise, like bright blue skies embracing us in ever-lasting warmth and loving light, the feeling of pure, euphoric joy repeated in a millionth of a thousand new beginnings, of experiences that have not yet tainted the perfection of the immaculate moment.

He had always felt an aversion to and a great anxiety in the presence of the formless and unrestrained. It symbolized forgetting oblivion, and the sheer shapelessness and measurelessnes of it all distressed a mind already so taken aback by deep existential thoughts and ruminations on the metaphysical and transcendent. For although he had already had one foot firmly grounded in the world of dreams, – these dreams occupying the space of outer spatial realms –, these were conceived, contained and safely concealed behind and within the inner boundaries of the mind. It brought him always back to the uncanny notion that perhaps even the unrestrained has its physical limits, that everything is contained within the other, within an outer sphere; the mind within a body within a planet within a galaxy within a universe ad infinitum.

He was frighteningly drawn by, and not immune to, the magnetic pull of the Moon on the tide, sinisterly sensitive to the slightest fluctuations of the gravitational pulls, climactic shifts and interplanetary drifts, of the colliding forces of Moon and Earth, of powers far beyond his control. Alone he was proof that an undeniable, inexorable and inextricable connection exists between all things living and the phenomena of the universe. He was especially affected by the colder, darker months; endured a laming of those powers that only the intense and powerful warmth and light of the Sun of the long and spirit-sustaining days of summer can enliven. He always found it hard to fathom how human beings were at all able to function during the periods in which cold and darkness had cast their cursed spell over the earth and wished that he, not unlike the various other variegated creatures of the forest, could summon himself into a long, deep sleep and awaken at the first thawing of the snow and the frozen soil of the earth; hoped with every fiber of his being and all the essence of his dying soul in winter that the prodigal Sun would once again return and, if for even just a brief, miniscule moment, look down upon him and show compassion on his wretched soul.

Only youth is impervious to the harsh, cold and unfavorable conditions of the colder months and discover endless possibilities for exploration in the abundant snow, snow banks, icy ponds and rivers, which became sledding slopes and ice rinks, snowballs and snow castles. But for Lucas, the fall into a deep state of melancholy coincided with precisely the point of transition from the fall of his childhood to the winter of ripe adulthood when winter became a dreadful, eternal struggle of his dying will after the novelties of careless, juvenile play under the summer Sun had subsided. He had spent the summer of his youth in wistful carelessness, fully unprepared for the hardships of the impending winter, so that when it all came falling down; when winter's drought dried up the joy of summer's sweet abound, he was left exposed and utterly vulnerable to winter's merciless attack. It was no wonder then that he, when the Sun had finally emerged from her eternal sleep and claimed her rightful throne, underwent a wonderful metamorphosis and resurrection of his vital senses, which, after months of tyrannical suppression, claimed their vengeance and exploded with all the thunderous and fiery passion of a newborn star. One could scarcely imagine that there could be light after the dark, and the thick blanket of ominous dark, gray clouds that hovered unwaveringly over the winter sky seemed eternal, if only it were not by virtue of some inner instinct buried deep within the human mind that told him to hold on, to just bear through another day, another week, another month, he would surely have perished. There was no in between, no moderation, no spring or fall with him, but only summer and winter, the extremities of two drastically opposing poles. They were a perfect analogy for the antithesis of his inner and outer being, the highs and the lows. The winter months provided a catalyst for the darker forces of his soul, and the summer months, – the creative, the joyful.

Staleness of life, of soul had brought him to this place in which he had for the duration of four years taken up residence. Although it quite resembled, in the disparate coolness of climate and temperament, the place and the people he had left behind, it might just as well and all the same have been endless light years away from home. But that was good, was what he had always wanted; a place so far, or far enough at least, that he could distance himself from that crippling affliction of heart, of soul that he had his entire life so desperately sought to escape. The source of this sudden move remained, much like his very existence, his every action; inarticulate, ambiguous, vague; naturally most undesirable qualities in a system in which everything had its predetermined place, its prescribed purpose. Thinking that he could find in this part of the world more of his kind, others who, like he, possessed that deeper philosophical understanding of the world, a place that had not yet borne the insidious mark of materialism to the degree that it had in the place of his upbringing. He searched everywhere, but could not find others like him who shared that similar unique disposition toward the light. He settled quickly into the humdrum of life there, coming all to soon to the disillusionment that life is much the same everywhere. But the novelty of a new place, a new start, a new language, was, as short-lived as it was, in the beginning, – always the beginning –, pure joy, excitement, adventure. It set his heart aglow and revived in him for an all too brief but nonetheless symbolic moment a spark of hopeful optimism. And he learned that chance, fate, destiny, – whatever one may wish to call it –, manifests itself in the most felicitous ways. He belonged nowhere really, felt nowhere quite at home; was convinced that there was not a place on this planet in which he would ever truly belong. And, being as indeterminate as he was and so often lamed by that necessary call to action that those insignificant and drudging daily duties required of him, he let fate unhindered and uncontested her unsteady course take. And indeed, he found life most pleasing when he simply allowed himself to be carried by the current. He was, when it all came down to it, never really certain as to what degree chance and destiny had played in his life, as fate was not in the slightest untouched by the insurmountable obstacles within the current system, obstacles that made the attainment of even the most minute of tasks a desperate battle.

Almost immediately upon his arrival in this northernmost imperial city of islands, where the people are all too tepid, cool and reserved, he took up study in the subject of modern literary theory at the local university. Enduring the tedious struggle in the darker months, after the very last bright yet still somehow sullen colors of autumn had begun to vanish, when the leaves had loosened their weakened grip from the frail branches to which they in summer so vigorously clung, he managed still somehow to muster the very last strands of his abysmally sparse and ever-waning strength to bring to an end a dreadfully long thesis on the most trivial, yet for the times, nonetheless most relevant of subjects, namely, on the nature of art, decadence and aestheticism in a literary classic, to be more exact, on the eternal conflict between inner and outer beauty; between a conception of life that grounds itself on a wholehearted adherence to the realm of the physical and one of an appreciation of inner, spiritual beauty. Laborious delays and difficulties in the completion of this work were countless and in large part attributed to his withering will in winter, so that it was a significant feat in itself that he, despite such obstacles, still managed somehow to see it through, especially since it was, in the end, all of it, to him nothing more than a distraction, insignificance, a mere temporary means through which to bide the time. And time he spent with inflated currency. For it wasn't real, none of it was real. Time was a fiction, a damning illusion. And nothing really mattered. That was, in fact, the dubious premise on which he had always lived, the burning candle beside which he in weary and restless hours allegiance to deep, precarious pondering pledged.

His mentor was a proper and prim woman from that place in the east that six ten years behind cemented partition and thorned wall divided stood. Untypically austere for her age, with her premature gray, coarse and brittle hair, she gave the appearance of one far beyond her years. But this did so please him, for he saw comforting wisdom in her countenance. The relationship between them throughout the two and some odd year mentorship remained, however, contrary to what he had anticipated, all too formal, professorial, dispassionate. It was only after the completion of the term of mentorship and the receipt of a Magister Artium that he was able to fully appreciate the stringent structure and order that had been imposed upon him in these years. And when it was all over, it, as with any exploit he had ever undertaken, left him fully and utterly bereaved and impoverished of his vital, inner strengths. But still, he cherished and hung on the wall that physical symbol of his pride; a testimony in pristine eggshell white, thick and grainy paper framed majestically in deep burgundy and frosted gold.

He had during the entirety of these four years taken up room and board in the pent house flat of a retired ambassador and professor emeritus, a self appointed aristocrat, who devoted excruciating diligence daily to scrutinizing the international press with ever so meticulous care, a routine that was only intermittently interrupted by incessant mumblings about the decay of the kingdom, the disintegration of the aristocracy and the mediocrity of the lower classes. He was a marvelous parody, if anything, of the upper classes for which he proudly stood. Residing in the heart of this city's infamously moneyed district, Lucas found himself during these fleeting years sheltered from the signs of the uncivilized mediocrity of the proletariat, to which he himself purportedly, and in the eyes of the ambassador, belonged, and of which the ambassador had so often warned; forced himself to suffer the branding flames of elitism and arrogance spewed from the mouth of this man so diabolical, so merciless in his condemnations, this man so intent on crushing any last morsel of his hopeful optimism. Lucas became accustomed, but never immune, to his slurs to the likes of "imbecile" and "miscreant," suffered, sacrificed and suppressed his freedom in tiny, life-expending increments. "You're an idealist, a hopeless dreamer, my boy," the ambassador would often say. "The world is no place for a dreamer like you." Lucas couldn't say that those words didn't sting. From the mouth of this man, he received them like a damning verdict against and striking negation of all the hopes he had built up daily, reduced them to the mere musings of a naïve youth, a foolish idealist, a dilly-dallier; banned his daily dreams and hopes to oblivion, so that it remained a daily battle for him to build back up and to reconstruct with each day anew the shattered shreds of his dignity. All he had left were dreams. He dreamt when it so pleased him. And so he did. He dreamt by night, he dreamt all day, he'd have dreamt his little life away if he could.

The entire lot was damned, in fact; degenerate and lifeless; sterile and stale to the core in the stench of unbearable snobbery, arrogance and insensitivity, all so marvelously masqueraded by a charading farce of finely trimmed hedges, Champs-Élysées-esque promenades, linden trees and opulent imperial structures. They were soulless souls, all of them; terribly bored with their own boredom, victims of their own passive indifference. And so he lived in these years, two feet in two disparately opposing and colliding worlds lightly planted. He bent and compromised his pride and principles, conformed as best he could; sold himself, – as all too many had become accustomed to doing in this system. He did what he had to do to get by, to see his needs met, and the sheltering comfort that he had found in the ambassador's stern but safe embrace was, in his eyes, a necessary evil; a means to his end.

And not too late, not too soon, – at that precise moment at which the planets and the stars in the most fortuitous fashion align, the ambassador's health had begun to drastically decline. A sudden laming of the body and mind that most of such ripe age afflicted, confounded by a serious ailment of the blood, had left the poor man unable to carry out the daily political and academic duties that he had for years so effortlessly carried out and that he had perceived so demanded of him. And so, quite naturally, it happened that time and circumstance had thrown, or rather, gently bestowed upon

Lucas, the custodial commission of caretaker, an undertaking which he readily accepted, for he felt indubitably indebted to the professor for the invaluable mentorship, security and wisdom he had imparted on him in the few but symbolic years that he had spent under his guidance. Grossly unaccustomed to this new role and inapt for the taxing duties it demanded of him, he was now, for the very first time in his life, left accountable, had someone depending on him. For the twelve months that followed, he became close kin to the decrepit, the decaying; saw hope in slow and painful traces seep from the ambassador's thin envelope of flesh, promising, threatening, dangling always imminent death before him; saw the light of a once vital and fiercely burning flame grow ever weaker. The entire experience would infiltrate the nervy flesh of Lucas' gentle heart until he would grow to learn, to see with his own eyes, the dark and gloomy; the unperfumed and unconcealed side of life.

Months like fleeting seconds flew, and with them, an era. And he, the ambassador, the professor, the doctor of philosophy, the feeble, old man was gone. They say that time heals the pain, but the present is all that Lucas felt, all that he had. With the ambassador's passing came it all crumbling. Then fear and great uncertainty of what lie ahead. Never before had he felt so ill prepared, never so abandoned. And how quickly he forgot the humiliation and degradation he had suffered at his hand. On the night of his passing, he heard; heard his voice call out his name that still and silent night. He searched the place in quiet steps but not a soul in sight. In rare moments he had shown to him what from others he concealed, and through a gentle hand, a gentle word, his gentle soul revealed. One last shattering shake from that furious force of grief would leave the ground beneath him for still a short while rumbling, until he, through shattered remnants and rubble of his sorrow stumbling, would find his way. Earth shuddered, and on the last night of a month of mourning, he, still mourning, weeping, slowly fell into deep sleep, and in sleep still half weeping, he waited, – waited until dawn, child of the morning, with her crimson cheeks, awoke and scattered her soft, sparkling light over the clear blue skies, in this instance in time in which the axis of Earth is most inclined toward her majesty, the Sun.

From the sweet relief of long, long

night awakening, he arose. His heart was brushed by some sudden and unsettling panic as he awoke from a dream of things that seemed so ancient, but that yet still materialized as the moment crept. Captured now by some present worry, some new and more pressing angst, he walked cautiously, cold feet on cold, creaking floor, down the narrow stairwell to the lower level of the flat on which the ambassador had often dwelled to explore the cause of his grief. And quickly, a calm, unsettling quietude fell upon this outer realm of inner spaces, unlike any other he had before experienced. For a moment, he forgot his former grief; felt now somehow strangely bereaved of that most primordial of all human instincts of want and need. Hesitantly through the bedroom window peeking, he spied a union of quite unearthly forms, – fantastic walking dreams; long legged beasts, stagger softly under long, thin blankets of white, cotton cloud. They seemed to be surveying with haunting care the sun-drenched meadows and forest fields of splendid green that soaked up the brilliant, warm, golden embrace of the morning light. The encapsulating warmth of the rising Sun touched the physical and spiritual senses and awoke the varied creatures of this weary world from their unconscious sleep, for there was nothing to which her resplendent light did not give budding life. And, as her light far over near meadows and dandelion fields slowly crept, thought he: what wonders of the inner soul that sing of the unspoken joys that might unfold, the adventures that await on the brink of something truly magical, wonderful.

Fourth Chapter

Having now fully arisen from this most unusual of sun-filled Sunday mornings, Lucas allowed himself quite effortlessly and indifferently now to be diverted from the greatest of improbabilities. Freed and unfettered by that conspicuous contract that had bound him to the ambassador, summoned by the rising Sun, he entered into the glistening streets in order to investigate and explore the curious unknown, – those entrancing sounds that had called to him from his dream, set his vital senses ablaze and rekindled in him now sweet memories of his youth and that old, dormant, abandoned and long forgotten fervor that inhabits the hearts of those who have not yet grown weary of the ceaseless wonders of this world. An eerie quietude prevailed out here too; all those common, assaulting sounds of progress that had incessantly, relentlessly worked day and night, night and day to keep everything in constant, unceasing motion simply disappeared. He saw, he heard now not a vehicle moving, not a truck transporting, not a factory chimney fuming, not a plane above flying, no garbage trucks hauling, no digital devices ringing, transmitting, – just those sweet sounds that sang from afar.

And so ensued a few short and everlasting hours of idle wander in the front street adjacent to the uniform column of trim and tightly stacked, light-pastel yellow, peach and green colored houses. He remembered a time long ago when car tires, fences and rusty coils; old, new and antiquated objects; dilapidated doohickeys and thingamajigs, as if touched by a brush of magic, had, in youth, just before the advent of those distracting devices, been transformed into the subjects of scrutinizing inspection, had become a fulfilling source of wonder in the sweeping hours before the fall. His careless whim was halted only by a further titillating curiosity of the prospect of what infinitely greater wonders awaited him in the vast fields beyond the bounds of this limited sphere. He felt a faint inclination to stay, but the source of that which had once held him there was no more, and the memory of yester night's mourning seemed now as old and as long forgotten as the ancient words contained in the books in the old professor's study. It occurred to Lucas that the vast planes beyond might hold endless possibilities and prospects he hadn't yet seen.

And what was home in the face of this new adventure, anyhow?

He was innocently intoxicated by the thought that the most recent happenings were somehow a product of his own imagination, a trick of the mind, a manifestation of his deepest dreams, – or worries –, and he could not help but think that he himself were perhaps the fruition, the conjured dream of a greater force vastly beyond his recognition. But it was real, was true living experience, no less than dreams are the symbolic revelation of the physical phenomena that we experience in our waking state. Whatever it was, it filled him always, and particularly now, with an unbound curiosity to explore that which, after what would have been, could have been, a simple day's trivialities under the Sun, had led to the most unusual turn of events in these waking hours. He was afraid, yet curiously drawn, to the distant but ever so present humming harmonies that emanated from the vicinity of those mysterious beasts and that disembodied and dispersed throughout the sun-silk summer sky. An orchestra of collective voices sounded, now with an even far greater degree of intensity; they echoed sweet songs of youth, enchanting trills and chimes, spectral voices, ping-pong pulses and lunar bounce that reverberated through the bountiful seas of trees, so distinct and captivating that all things crawling felt themselves compelled to peak their heads through the margins of marshes, meadows, mossy stones, trees and brooding backwaters, as if in a moment of dazed contemplation of and complicity with this strange song.

And beckoned, distracted once more, he could hear the long-legged beasts that roamed the valleys and that seemed to have carried with them the alluring song of some enchanting spell that was most pleasing to the ear and that once heard, left one wanting for more and wishing that it would never abate. It was the most beautiful and ingenious progression of musical notes that one could ever have fathomed, arranged in such a precise manner so as to produce a melody far unmatched, far unparalleled by anything his ears had ever beheld. Not every possible combination of every melody ever conceived by man since the beginning of time could produce such a wondrous succession of sounds that of the trance of the heavens sang. Lucas had, however, not been untouched by the curious sentiment enlivened by this music before. There was something in that music that was still yet somehow strangely familiar to him; it was as if he had known it, heard it, dreamt it somewhere, sometime before in the distant corners of his manifold mind, in the deepest depths of his incandescent dreams. He welcomed it, not like the way in which one welcomes a stranger or a mere acquaintance, but like a dear friend you once knew, whom you had long since not seen, but with whom you had after years once again been reunited. It was ominous, sent chills through his opened soul and left him for a brief spell trembling in trepidation. It moved him, violated the senses, the flesh. For the first time in his life, he felt so vilified, so alive, so real! Everything was real and, for the very first time, the fuzzy, inarticulate and vague state of his mind came into focus, solidified, became coherent; multiplied and amplified the reception of these sounds, unified the senses in perfect, synthesized harmony. A message, a warning was contained in and carried by these mesmerizing melodies, intended for him and him alone. And he received it. It proclaimed end, beginning; it promised resurrection and retribution; it cried come, follow and seek out the source that calls to you before the setting of the Sun.

The message imbued him sudden meaning and purpose, signified a call to duty, a mission. This sounding of the most incomprehensible composition of melodies delighted him immeasurably and fulfilled him, like an opiate, with an unbound desire to seek out and more intimately acquaint himself with the source of that distant choir of child-like voices that fused with the earth-shaking thuds and thumps of these elephantine creatures as they stumbled softly by.

Having ended his inspection of the district, it became frighteningly clear to Lucas that he was the only one in the discernable vicinity who remained. And so, he felt himself forced to abandon the safe and comforting confines of his familiar dwelling and to set out even further along the sandy paths and dirt roads that surrounded this suburban settlement. He had not far to go until he reached a nearby monument, a small fortress previously bustling with busy traffic and by-passers, now an abandoned box of steel and cement amidst a field of silver, gold and rusted copper scrap metal; the compiled, compressed and composted residuum of progress amidst this silver, gold and copper scrap metal marshland. But they shined! They reflected the light of the Sun like jewels. He heard, he remembered the busy bustle of cars, the streets and the crowds. The synthetic gray of the withered construction flaunted its own special, aberrant kind of beauty; took on magnificent proportions in the amplifying light of the mid-morning Sun, the shadows of which mimicked an abstraction of fascinating geometrical shapes and patterns formed by the sharp, imposing scrap metal fragments. The contrast between the stark symmetry of the synthetic construction of the scrap metal heaps and the surrounding formless, shapeless and untamed organic element contributed to the formation of the image of an at once abandoned, uncultivated and desolate wasteland; conjured a fantastic mirage, at once unsettling and exhilarating, of a world that now, within the blink of an eye, had irrevocably ceased to exist. It reminded him that everything has its place and that beauty too springs from the most unlikely and improbable of sources.

Only slight hunger, aroused by what had now amounted to several hours of exploration, and the prospect of an indeterminate journey ahead, an enticing interest in what abandoned, unguarded treasures might be contained therein, but more the need to find someone with whom to share the experience of the morning light, provoked him to enter. He found an abandoned space. A few cautious and hesitant shouts confirmed his suspicions and filled him now with great unease. He raided the shelves with an urgency guided only by the slight fear of being observed or caught, filled his rucksack to the rim with some Sunday morning treasures and rushed out like a mischievous thief, a soldier, a pirate drunk with affirmation and satisfaction of his crime and conquest. This newly acquired nourishment would surely sustain him for a considerable stretch of the impending journey, for the spirit shrinks and shrivels in the face of carnal necessity and fine thoughts and philosophies are the rare luxury of the warm, rested and physically sustenant.

As he fled, he was startled to the heavens by a stone that recoiled off of a massive metal cylinder that lie not a few meters from him. A young boy of about eight or so appeared from high atop the highest metal heap, steel rod raised in hand. The piercing light of the Sun reflected ferociously from all angles onto the scrap metal mountain, created a contortion of clashing reflectors, blinded Lucas for a moment, causing him to shield his eyes. Blinding light became shadow as another boy peered his head out from inside a towering crane that hung ominously over him like a monstrous hand. Others, about ten or twelve in number, also of the seemingly similar approximate age, emerged now from concealment. Lucas found himself suddenly surrounded and sequestered by this most unwelcoming band of youths. The circle parted. One of the youths stepped forward and presented himself as the superior of the group. "How come they didn't take you?" asked the brazen boy in a manner most disagreeable with and unwelcoming to Lucas. However seemingly simple, this question revealed to Lucas that the youth had been more informed than he as to the peculiar happenings of the morning light. Confused, still quite startled and knowing not quite how to respond, he paused for an indeterminate moment, then countered with a question: "Have you seen the beasts?" The great inquisitiveness of the others of the group caused them to come closer until Lucas found himself now locked in a tight, impenetrable enclosure. "You're not supposed to be here," spoke the youth. "There must be a reason," he continued. The look of total confusion on Lucas' face prompted the militant youth to further remark: "Don't you know? They've taken the elders; all of them. Each and every last one." "How do you know this?" inquired Lucas. "We saw it with our own eyes. They're waiting for us. Over there," remarked the boy. He pointed to a structure far, far off in the distance. "We're not going there. They want us to forget. If we go, they'll make us forget," he remarked further, now in a somewhat frightened, foreboding and anxious tone. "They've taken the elders and spared the youngest," he concluded.

They saw them appear in the dead of night. The beasts turned topsy-turvy every single stone to ensure that they had carried out their divine device. To execute their scheme, they had to ensure that not one had been left unaccounted for. With precision they probed and infiltrated the inner spheres of our human hearth. Some strange essence that they exhumed consumed the banished ones, devoured them whole, — those fading faces in the wake of the fall who had wandered within the realm of confining walls; gazes dissected; run into wide-open spaces, they looked into faces, waited for a sign. One by one, they began to fall; they wondered, they worried in despair at it all. They had no idea, not the slightest clue; only a few of the perceptive ones of them knew. What did they think, what did they feel? Did they cry for their children, did they doubt it was real? Was it happening, was it true, could it happen this way? Did they heed the words the wise men say? There was nothing that any pleading or fighting could do. The youths revealed to Lucas that all artificial means of contact had by now been fully severed and word had spread among and between the loosely dispersed and scattered tribes of younglings that no sign of the elderly remained. They were informed that they were to make their way to designated posts where instructions were to be received as to the next step in the execution of the divine plan, the transition into the next phase.

Creatures, wonderful apparitions of the most varied kind brushed the land as far as the human eye could see. They seemed all the while to be ominously searching, spying, surveying the land, and it was unbeknownst to Lucas that they had all the while been casting ever so often a watchful eye on him. What was the purpose of this work about which they so carefully went? thought he. Were they seeking out those who may have gone unapprehended upon their arrival? What precisely had happened to the elders? What was to become of those who remained, those who had for some unknown and unspoken reason been spared? Surely, they too would inevitably grow old with time. Would not the same fate with which the elders had been met too befall the younglings when the time came? And once more, he thought deeper. What greater purpose did the inescapable fate of the process of physical decline that afflicted every living thing and that inevitably manifests itself in the senseless, denigrating dissolution of our physical and mental faculties serve? Lucas pondered on the inability, yes, even the unwillingness of his kind to deeply and significantly reflect on such essential questions of time and space, of the critical metaphysical matters pertaining to our existence; to delve into the deepest recesses of the mind, to question the conditions of a life that is at once so insignificant yet so inconceivably and unfathomably profound. Had they not revealed to them the rare and precious gift bestowed upon our kind of reflexivity and reflection into the conditions, contradictions and peculiar premises of our existence? So many questions remained unanswered. But as always, it was such questioning that had separated Lucas from the mindless drones of unthinking masses, and he thought that the lack of ascension to such thoughts must have been the ultimate result of some tragic cosmic flaw, some infelicitous deficit in the mind of most.

Fifth Chapter

Lucas ventured now deeper into the forests, barges, dry grassy thickets, dams, streams and ponds of his abound. Momentary lapses of delightful diversion were disturbed only by a gradual magnification of the sounds he had this morning so unfalteringly welcomed. They carried but now a dismal, ill-boding tone. He sought refuge in such moments in concrete tunnels; in huge, hollow, mossy tree trunks and caves, or in any other means of concealment that offered themselves to him when the fear had overcome him. Fright, however, did not prevent him from peeking out through the corners of his confines every now and then. In one instance, he was suddenly swept aback as he experienced with his own eyes two infinitely long and sinewy legs that flowed like loose, elastic and electrical cables in the most splendid, soft and slow dispatch of movements. The creature was composed of what appeared to be a synthesis of organic flesh and something of the mechanical in nature. What dazzling wonder did he behold as he saw other creatures strangely familiar surveying the land; forms yet unformed, unconjured, unshaped by the disheveled and dissembled mind, so untraceably irreconcilable with anything the human mind could infer. The image of what seemed like a white ivory porcelain visage protruded from a cloudy, charcoal gray configuration formed of seemingly similar undistinguishable features. Formless arms and formless legs extended from this formless form. Above, a migrating formation; a sweeping stream of equally strange figures flowed in seeming haste toward a common destination. In the watchful gaze of these creatures, Lucas saw the image of his mind's internal eye reflected back at him, felt himself accused and deeply affected, distinctly dissected, apart from them, yet somehow strangely in and of them. A strange, strange sensation indeed as illusion became real, became experience; waking and walking dream in these hours before the fall.

The creatures were earth incarnate, nature soberly awoken, turned into abundant, bursting life and plenteous profusion, resurrected after ages of oppression. So too was the structure that they of earth and light force forged. At its base, four gargantuan legs sprouted like roots from the earth. The distances alone in the space between the long and lanky limb-like columns of the structure were absolutely immense and spanned across the entire breadth of the forest. The brown, wooden like base of the columns were like massive tree trunks that seemed to fuse with the forest landscape, camouflage themselves in its colors, so that they quite seemed to be in and of the forest. The base of the structure, much resembling the green shrubbery and flora of the forest, extended all the way up to an arc-shaped head. Standing motionless, wonderfully awe-stricken by the sight of this monstrously and stupendously spectacular thing, Lucas was frightened for a moment by the realization that he had made his presence known. But, several of the creatures, gazing benevolently now at him for a brief yet significant moment, gave a subtle, but penetrating signal of their acceptance of his presence before continuing their intentful surveillance. It was somehow uncannily impossible to ascertain the size and proportions of the structure in relation to the surrounding landscape, such that Lucas was fully unable to discern whether it was close or far, much like the way in which the Moon, the Sun and the stars sometimes appear in almost tangible distance from us as we look up into the skies above, so much so, that we feel that we could almost touch them and would chase after them forever were it not for the confining force of our finitude, of Earth's gravitational pull. In the same way, the physical presence of the structure seemed somehow to have defied any method or law of spatial inference altogether, so that it was impossible for Lucas to ascertain its actual proximity with relation to him. He quivered, crouched, pressed his knees so tightly against his chest that he could scarcely breathe, as this behemoth of a creature, now apparently oblivious to his presence, passed by and then continued on its way.

The licentious music of the morning had now temporarily ceased to work on his delicate senses and the verity of the situation at hand hit him like thunder. Scarcely had he obtained any essential answers as to the recent happenings. He thought of mother and father, came quickly to the assumption, – now turned more into a certain probability –, that even they were gone. Fitting into the mood, – the state of survival for which the situation called, he mourned them here and now; quickly and silently gave his farewell. He, even after realizing that his presence had been altogether dismissed by the creatures, thought it still best to wait until they were sufficiently out of sight to make the slightest of movements and cautiously continue his journey. Coerced by fear to action, he mustered the strength he needed and continued his excursion forward until he deepened himself far, farther and soon irretrievably deeper into the bushy green plains ahead that marked the division between the industrial landscape of the city outskirts and a receding jungle of green fields reaching as far as the eye could see.

After several hours of travel, he reached the edge of a creek. The ferocious intensity of the mid-day Sun, which illuminates all things and inspires enlightened elucidation, began to lame the mind, to cause restless resignation, beckoned him to sleep. Reclining in the cool, calming shadows of the forest's trees, he lay to rest his heavy head for a brief eternity. A deep, deep sleep befell him. Dreams brought him back to his childhood, to a time when the discoveries of youth are never-ending, adventures always unfolding. He remembered how he had, as a child, been drawn to the seductive, anesthetizing scent produced by the mixture of the tar of the street and the blaring, humid heat of the mid-afternoon summer Sun. He envisioned pink bubble gum and riddles in bubble gum wrappers; giant bubble mouthed bullfrogs, grasshoppers and preying mantises in the creek behind the house of his childhood. Before the threshold of the creek lie an army of bright, yellow dandelions and translucent white wishing weeds. For a brief moment, he questioned if it were all real or just a flaw in his perception, a glitch in that perplexing mechanism of mind that sets memories in motion. Was that which remained mere scattered fragments, that which later lingered in the mind as recollection just a lingering afterthought of something he had once experienced in a fantastical dream? Blowing on the fine and fluffy; soft and satin-like threads of at least one or two or more of the dandelions, – these spectacular things –, had become a necessary ritual, a paramount stage in the monumental initiation of youth before entry into the creek, which was no less imperative than rubbing yellow dandelions on his chin and nose, which left him giggling with mischievous pleasure each time when he found, as if to his renewed surprise, sun-yellow stains on his nose, cheeks and chin. Amidst this perfect composition of summer's glow; of blue, yellow and green, – the motley colors of his dreams, he would revel in the sight of beautiful parachutes of dandelion snow, fine translucent feathers of dandelion seeds as they dispersed weightlessly up and into the lavender sky, danced in the gentle summer breeze and evaded him like unconsummated hope as he longingly and unfulfillingly tried to grasp them. He made crowns of the stems and sometimes even suckled on the bittersweet milk contained in them, which always left him with sticky hands and fingers. Here he was king of his castle, a royal of the child creek kingdom. Crossing the threshold of the creek was like entering into another world; one in which he could give full reign to his wildest musings. Marking the entry into this elysium was a steep, dirt-drenched slope on which lie a field of luscious, ripe red strawberries, enticing him to pluck and plunder them, leaving him always with a strange sense of guilty pleasure, as if he had done something forbidden, an act for which mother nature had punished him with ruby red lips and red finger tips. Strange what sometimes came, – the enervation that seemed always to have accompanied such childish explorations that ensued in the hours of refuge from the intense heat of the mid-afternoon summer

Sun into the cool and soothing shadows of colossal trees and weeping willows provided in the hidden recesses of the creek, during games of hide and seek and hush-hush peek, – they all elicited a sullen recognition of the finality and sweet tragedy of it all, for it always inevitably drew to an end, – bitter, sweet and sorrowed end. But oh how sweet that which he with wide eyes, ears and nose for that brief but all-enduring moment welcomed: Ladybugs, sweet honeybees; drumming herds of sweet humming birds appeared in tiny wet gorges. Precious, pebbled ponds illuminated brilliantly through small openings in the forest's thick brushes of lime green leaves, – tiny oases shimmering like golden-white glitter onto the serene and still mossy green and white waters. He reveled in the tickling, tantalizing sound of the water drops trickling into the pond from tiny waterfalls. Shiny, blazing blue, green and red dragonflies with their translucent wings were transformed into miniature helicopters, celestial ferries, – magical muses of the forest realm. He built forts, crossed little streams, hop-scotch hopped over cold stones, which he sometimes overturned to find a city of potato bugs, snails and slugs basking, concealing themselves in the cool, moist mud beneath, only to immediately restore them back to their original position out of some fear of disturbing this natural habitat or somehow breaking the unwritten laws of nature. Funny how such acts of foresight attribute themselves solely to youth. Why is it that those riper in years seem to have forgotten or broken this sacred code, this primal unity with nature? Only contrived culture makes one grow impervious to the juvenile joys of youth. In our older years, the magical mysteries of the world seem to evade us and we lose the will to dream, to wonder.

And in the midst of this splendid summer dream, June bugs jumped from branch to branch. Bumblebees suckled on the sweet pollen of the fragrant flowers – lilac, purple, white and blue. Ladybugs basked on the lime green water-lily pads of the tepid pond, resting in summer sunlight's splendor. Flower pedals sprouted electric blue butterfly wings that floated up and through phosphorescent rays of light that penetrated through the sparse openings of the trees and the leaves, and he remembered in this precise moment that nothing is as it seems, nothing is or ever will be as it now is, as it once was; thought of the constant and ever-moving transition and metamorphosis of all things living. Entranced by the singular beauty of this exquisite image, his eyes sprouted wings, his mind, his soul were filled with the most fervent zeal to experience through all of the vital senses, to feel at once all of life's countless wonders in the immediate instance of the present moment, to make the most joyful moment forever linger. But he realized that the limited realm and time of the space that we inhabit is far too infinitesimal, far too miniscule, far too insufficient to ever possibly reveal all of the endless elements of life's ever unfolding tapestry of visions and memories that constantly elude us. It awoke in him now the unwavering wish about which he every night while into sleep falling mused, – the wish to fire with sun-sparked rage and unbound fury the world that held him; to expound every binding wall; to repel every imposing thing that finds its form in the confining masses that govern this earthly sphere; to transcend the weighted and weightless, at once forever and nothingness of time; to taste the sorrow-spirited tears that would flow from a glimpse of the essence that precedes and surpasses it; to touch the see-through skies; fly through the infinite realm of star-crossed spaces; to embrace the secret melody that sings of what was and will be throughout the endless years. A twinkle of bright, hopeful optimism brushed him like fire as he thought of how fortunate he was and what an incomparable and immeasurable gift it is to behold even a miniscule moment, yes, even a minute particle of the bountiful beauty and wonders the earth holds, and that moments and visions such as these are all too scarce and too few and far in between. But, when they do appear, they reveal themselves to us in the most extraordinary ways, give us in brief and incremental fragments a taste of sweet eternity.

Stifling hunger awoke him. A handful of wild berries offered themselves to him at this moment as the only reasonable means of sustenance. He could have thought of a million more pleasing alternatives, some even far less pleasing, but it was imperative that he restore those mental faculties that equilibrium of mind and good temper foster, for fine thoughts and philosophies are the privilege of the well nourished. Crouching on his knees at the edge of a pond, cupping his hands together, he reached forward to fetch some water in order to quench his thirst, to steal some refreshing relief from the brutal and life-expending heat of the mid-afternoon summer Sun. He forgot his thirst, beheld his likeness now in the glimmering surface of the shallow water. The trees and the Sun framed fantastically the image of his form, which materialized before him with such lucidity. That which he beheld was an image unforged, unfiltered, naked, clean and pure, illuminated by nature's candid and brazen light. He saw a worried, but wise forehead, two heavy but hopeful eyes, saddened, sorrowed and sympathetic; a nose; unsymmetrical and slightly overbearing for his frail face, but strong and noble; and thin, soft lips that could not feign sadness, no matter how hard he tried and in spite of the fact that he had scarcely a reason to be happy. He recognized himself here, now, for the very first time; saw in disappointment behind his frail, sinewy frame, soft and weak, his soul; surrender, timid resignation, anger, anxiety, and most apparent of all, fear. Although he had matured exceedingly in mental stature, he had still never quite fully grown into his body. It was uncertain if his full-pledged protest against the inequity of the process of debilitating age had lent him the appearance of one significantly younger in years, for there remained in his visage a surprising bearing of youth, a youthful countenance that concealed too well the hardships he had endured, so that it was indeed a wonder that he preserved, in spite of these, still a bright sparkle of hopeful, child-like naiveté. Entranced by his own image on the surface of the water, he recognized here and now, however, hardly the slightest semblance, barely an inkling of recognition of the child he once was. What blasphemous trickery! What treacherous deception by the hands of time!

He was drawn to deeper questions yet. Was our perception of the world only as real as that made visible by its reflection? thought he. For the perception of all objects was altered by the degree, angle, intensity and direction in which the light cast itself upon them; was the result of an interplay of light and shadow that showed us an incalculable number of infinitely different and varied versions, impressions and interpretations of the apparent. It was no wonder then that things appeared more pleasing to the eye in the dawn and dusk of day when the light of the Sun had shone ever so dimly, not too brightly and not too weakly, and rendered the disproportionate; the stark and offending imperfect somehow softer, more tempered. That is why the light is as damning as it is redeeming, as deceptive as it is true, for it, while revealing in resplendent light the beauty of all things manifest, also makes painfully visible the fleshy nature and truth of all that upon which we cast our eyes. Beautiful beguilement! So, our perception of the objects of this world is something so flexible, so easily manipulated and fractured by the constantly fluctuating patterns of the moment's light, such that the image is from moment to moment never quite identical. He pondered further on the nature of physical beauty and how the Sun illuminates and makes visible the phenomena of this world and realized that there was an inverse relationship, – a marvelous and most whimsical interplay between our spiritual, physical and mental perception of beauty. How complex the faculty of vision and what a gift it is to perceive the multitudinous array of shades and colors, the unfathomable richness of the universe's endless color schemes. He thought; he remembered how all earthly objects must be the imperfect, finite reflection of a transcendent reality and that the objective of life must be, ideally, to achieve rational perception of the immutable ideas in incremental recollections of an original absolute knowledge buried deep within the mind. We progress through the mistaken belief, so a wise philosopher once said, that the apparent is real, to a recognition that true from stands behind the imperfect worldly image, to a perception of abstract or mathematical shapes, and finally, to full apprehension of the fundamental ideas such as beauty, justice and goodness. A leaf floated slowly down from a vigilant tree above, gently touched the tranquil water, distorted the image, disturbed his careful inspection and brought him back to the moment.

Sixth Chapter

The path to the acquisition of the source of the sounds that had called to Lucas led him to the crumbling facade of what had once been a cathedral entangled now in winding vines that sprouted and penetrated from beneath and through its underlying foundation. Cracks revealed themselves in the ruins of this once magnificent and majestic construction of white marble, – once the opulent symbol of the earthly transcendent, of an autonomous deified force that had once demanded worship, surrender and ritual sacrifice. Up high, carved in stone, read the words "[…] a beautiful sunrise eternally." He observed various creatures gather in what appeared to be a silent communion, – a secret, sacred meeting of sorts. No words or sign of the interchange of words, – at least not in the manner to which humans are accustomed –, seemed to be taking place. The countenance of these creatures revealed nonetheless that they were transmitting, expressing and exchanging thoughts and intentions through some most strange means unknown and most unfamiliar to Lucas. The dialectic discourse was periodically and temporarily disturbed whereby several of the creatures directed a mysterious, benevolent glance toward him, yes, him, the one upon whom such diligence had seldom been bestowed. The glaring gaze of one of the creatures expressed to Lucas at once that he was not to feel threatened and revealed that that which was transpiring before his eyes was the devising of some greater, infinitely more profound plan. He saw a myriad of fates reflected in the deep, abysmal eyes of the creature and he felt a calm, soothing comfort in the feeling that he was under its safeguard, for its countenance gave comforting promise of allegiance. Others of the creatures, in the midst of the constant exchange of psychic transmissions, gazed with the most intent yet seemingly effortless demeanor of impassive indifference at the Sun. Others yet seemed to be guarding and surveying the elements of the surrounding landscape, which gave Lucas the resounding impression that they had been here before, that they had once commanded a dominion over this earthly sphere. In any case, it seemed indeed that they were no strangers here. The prospect appeared to Lucas now more than probable that his kind were in fact themselves only visitors and intruders in what had seemed to always have been a rightful realm belonging to these creatures, one to which they had now, after an eternity, once again returned.

This secret meeting of silent words lasted for what seemed like a small eternity and Lucas felt not the slightest divergence in his studious intrigue in this phantasmic spectacle, behind which lie a need to discern the cause of the curious behavior, nature, origins and intentions of these mystical creatures. A slight fear arose of the prospect that if he were to have made even the slightest movement, this would have somehow disturbed the delicate proceedings of the exchange. It occurred to him that the creatures had not at one single point throughout this entire deliberation reclined, recessed or faltered in their scrutiny, but that they had carried always the guarded gesture; stood always in an ever so charged posture of restless offense. It seemed that whatever was here taking place did not call for resignation, but elicited rather a constant, conscious awareness. There was no doubt in his mind that vital matters were being conceived in the intrinsic messages conveyed between the beasts, and he could not help but feel that the outcome of his own fate somehow lie inextricably implied in and connected with whatever conclusions were to be attained in their estimation. When he felt the moment most opportune, he abandoned his inspection of this sanctimonious summit of celestial souls momentarily, out of fear of outstaying his welcome, or perhaps of becoming too much privy to the nature of that which he had been observing, on the slight yet probable chance that the objective of the creatures was not as amicable as Lucas had anticipated.

The face of an immense, mammoth of a creature peered out now from behind the ruins of the withered and decayed facades of the cathedral. It itself seemed to be curiously inspecting, analyzing, gazing in inquisitive and confused wonder, as if entranced and intrinsically moved by this most external of outer constructs, so much so, that it seemed, for a brief and decisive moment, to have completely dismissed the presence of the wayfarer, who had, in turn, all the while been observing it. And then, it seemed to convey a sudden startling awareness of that which it had been observing, as if suddenly made privy to its meaning, its purpose. Finally suspending its inspection, apparently satisfied with having arrived at an answer to this baffling riddle, or perhaps even dismissing it for want of deriving at a logical answer, it focused its attention now fully on Lucas, accepting and affirming his presence, his existence as if it had been the most self-evident of factualities, as if it had known of his presence all along, had perhaps even sought him out. The creature donned a friendly, peaceful demeanor that was most agreeable with and welcomed by Lucas.

Then, suddenly, as if in the trampling transition of a fleeting dream, Lucas found himself kneeled before the creature on the steps of the foundation of the cathedral and could not by any means of any faculty of logical inference at his disposal deduce how this had come to transpire. He forgot. Entranced, he listened, he heard, he received the unspoken words that emanated from the image of this most venerable, pious and preeminent creature that seemed to convey themselves to him in the most abstract of forms. Its words were like music, were pure emotion and penetrated through means of the outer senses to the inner realm of his soul. "You see," spoke the creature, without uttering so much as a single word, "you are the essence of an idea yet unfulfilled, a mere shadow of the spark of the idea of your creator, to whom we refer as the Superlative, the last remnant of a dying star that once shone so bright, brighter than all the stars combined and with all the fiery passion that was once infinite source, youth and beginning. What you see before your eyes is the accumulation and culmination of an eternity of infinite progress and knowledge. Some day, you too will go, but the story will not end with you, for you are at once of and with one and every thing. Someone else will be there throughout the endless years. The eternal cycle of life for your kind reflects itself in the workings of the hour, the day, the turning of the seasons, the antinomy of light and dark; wake and sleep and of that which you call good and evil. Each holds within it a tiny inkling of the essence of time and existence. Yet time is so much more than you can fathom. It is almost impossible that your kind should conceive of time as anything but a linear construct. As surely as the Earth turns, the Sun rises and falls, so too is the nature of the evolution of your kind. Memories are what set you apart from the multifarious creatures on your planet, – and memory is nothing more than emotion, which, in turn, is the connecting thread of all creation. The state of being after your departure from the corporeal realm, – which has remained a riddle that has plagued your kind since the beginning of time –, if I shall put it in a manner most comprehensible to you, is something like the release of electric nodes of energy of the singular unit into the uniform nucleus of life creation; the transcendence of the transient, tangible substance into the intangible, unified whole. The universal unity is an infinitely intricate mechanism, – the harmonious connection, correlation and interrelation of individual parts; the never-ending systolic distension, accumulation and gathering of always new knowledge, which disperses, absorbs, collects, withdraws, only to again disperse. It is a never-ending process of trial and error, of striving toward sublime perfection of pure intellect and essence. Your planet is but a mere miniscule molecule, a single elemental cell in the anatomical anatomy of a vast universe of entities, a single verse within a universe within a multi-verse and so forth; it is the rhythmic flow and fusion of all matter and material, the blood line of all things animate and inanimate. Humankind is but a mere sliver in the grand scheme of things, and yet so much more. You are something like the busy bees constantly collecting the very pollen, the fruitful succulent nectar of the knowledge of life and creation, which, in turn, necessitates and facilitates, yes, perpetuates the reciprocal cycle of life, – a constant birth and rebirth."

The creature then spoke of the age-long vigilance of its kind over our kind, over our unavailing struggle on this planet; spoke of the fallacy of the ways of humankind, of the politics of human suffering, oppression and exploit. It spoke of the infinite wisdom of its kind and revealed to the entranced youth tiny inklings of the story of its own origins, of its purpose; schooled him on all things metaphysical; made him see with his soul's eye the resplendent nature of all things transitory and transcendental. Then came a chronicling of the events that had led to this meaningless and infinitely meaningful moment in the time and timelessness of the present now. The creature spoke of the great lack of humility and selfish pride with which we had held a finite flame to the institution of contrived, counterfeit, substanceless substance; spoke of creativity trampled by calculating, conspiring, scheming utility; spoke of the beguiling lure of the inanimate image that to us shallow sheen and idol became, of our transgressions against the infinite gifts and wonders of that which we call nature. He spoke of how his kind had always been there, had always watched over our kind in its restless journey toward the attainment of knowledge and progress. And next, it spoke the finest, most wonderful words; spoke of the eternal nature of the world and of all things living; of youth, rebirth and the source of all life; reminded the wayfarer, this blue and wide-eyed wonderer, that it is the resplendent warmth of the Sun to which we owe our physical and spiritual conception and propagation. It spoke of man's greatest fault, namely, his failure to harness the at once spiritually and physically regenerative forces embodied in her everlasting light. It spoke finally of the spiritual value placed by the elders on things of the mere physical realm, the reduction of the infinitely abundant and immutable gifts of nature to tangible means and substance. They traded these things, made value of the valueless, infinite of the finite. They forged in these things the fraudulent stamp of nature and held them in criminal pride up to worship, brought nature to its knees, enslaved that which they deemed inferior, inadequate and insufficient in the name of progress. "Creation cried eternal tears for you, – the tears you shed in dreams, in memories and in subtle, momentary glimpses into the true affection that only comes in moments of illumination, elucidation and clarity under the Sun."

The beast spoke further of the inconceivably infinite vastness of space and time, of the collective cry of all creation that had inevitably led to this significant moment; a tangible string of intangible particles containing within it an infinite imprint of the eternal. It assured Lucas that he ought not fear the present happenings, that he may forget the grief of the morning and delight instead in the prospect of that which were soon to follow. It revealed to him that the image of its own apparent likeness was but a physical manifestation of its true form, and that if Lucas or any of his kind were to behold the image of its kind, they would surely parish, for the light that they radiated was far too brilliant for the human eye to behold. So, they appeared to him, to his kind, in a form that was at once perceivable and comprehensible, most accessible and pleasing to him.

He was informed that small groupings of the younglings and others of the chosen ones, like him, to whom the instructive duty had been prescribed, were everywhere scattered throughout the outlying towns and forests, and that it lie before him the task of seeking them out by the end of the day's light, and that once he had found his way to his designated post, the phase of instrumentalization would commence. He was then pacified by the reassurance imparted by the creature that his fears were but the natural resurgence, – aftershocks of the former world, which would only naturally manifest themselves in precisely such unsettling worries and that this was only a necessary step in his journey toward the attainment of true understanding of the world. He likened the reaction of Lucas' kind to their new situation to that of an invalid to health, to that feeling of uncontainable exhilaration and overcompensation of energy and will that is restored in us after a debilitating and brash but brief sickness afflicts us, a renewed appreciation of the strength and vitality that makes us whole. It reassured him that they would watch over him always and that the common dangers and troubles of the day that were so commonplace in yesterday's world would become but a mere illusion in the new world that awaited, that they had in store for us.

This notion seemed unfathomable to Lucas, and although he had never directly experienced the trivial and troubling worries that had so often plagued so many others of his kind, it had been revealed to him, had become emotional experience by mere virtue of sentiment and memory. And the younglings, – they would become the freshly planted young seedlings, untainted yet by the toxic and poisonous virus of the lie of the way of life of those who preceded them.

And a final assurance came from the creature. "If you ever wish to call for us," it spoke, "sing, sing the music that comes from your heart and we will know. Music is the language of the soul, of the heavens. No other thing can so beautifully and more ideally capture its essence. It far exceeds all that which the other of the baser senses can behold. It is the intangible form of the tangible essence, the inner content behind the physical, form-given realm of time and space. Music is a fusion, – the harmony of melody and rhythm contained in notes, the transcendent trance and melody, two static poles working in unison to comprise the harmonious whole. It captures and contains the sorrows of humankind and sends them on soft, majestic wings up to the skies above.

So if you ever wish to call for us, just sing."
And in the very midst of this thought's
transmission, the message was terminated
and the creature gone.

Seventh Chapter

The mid day Sun had now aligned so perfectly in the centre of the wide and all-encompassing horizon. Starburst bright light shone with ever-greater intensity, became warmth and illuminating experience, now awakening and startling awareness and knowledge of the baffling secrets hidden behind the cool, concealing shadows of all earthly objects. The prospect of finding others who shared his similar fate, to impart unto them the wonders that he had since the unusual happenings of the early morning light experienced, did not give Lucas any considerable consolation. It was more so that his heart, despite the creature's recent reassurance, was filled with great fear and anxiety of the burden of the legacy now bequeathed him. Lucas rested his head for a short moment as the message on the metaphysical that he had from the creature received weighed heavily on his mind, on his soul. Remnants and ruins, visions of a distant and long forgotten time and place materialized now before him. He saw a massive jungle of gray concrete in the farthest reaches of the northern hemisphere, on that part in which Earth's northern axis is farthest removed from the Sun, a place he had never before seen, but that appeared to him now so starkly real. He saw intricate flakes of translucent, frosty white crystals descend slowly and slower from the iron sky. A gentle, invasive earthly wind whispered, warned and conspired through the naked, organic flesh of pale, thin and brittle barren branches. A thick matte blanket of lustrous, silvery white capped the landscape, muting all sound in tranquilizing tranquility. The distant dying Sun bade her last farewell, flickered like a dull, fading flame, fused, conformed to the ashen gray, white and ashen sky, sedated all hope and happiness. Creatures lay hidden in their burrows, immersed in winter's somber sleep. Even the tired earth, once warm, ample and fertile in the summer Sun, had forgotten her creatures and slept the eternal sleep. The naked Moon, friend of the lonesome, restless night, usurper of the Sun, surveyed the fruitless desert; cast its blanket of faint, feeble light over the deadened earth. He heard the collective voice of nature's slumbering creatures in shallow voices from shallow graves sigh. A gray-haired maiden, sad and sorrowed, with frosted breath spoke: "Slowly and slower winter's slow clock ticking, little by little from its frozen pond drinking, more and more it takes from me, summer's long forgotten memory, until I, deeper and deeper in this winter sleep falling, can remember no more, am myself no more." Heavy thuds and thumps reverberated through the icy plane with increasing rapture, threatened, broke the peaceful slumber of the forest's creatures, of winter's lulling lullaby. Cracks formed in the icy riverbank from whence the sounds appeared and spread through the thick, solid sheet of pale, cold ice. Hiding behind a wall of snow, he watched, he saw men masked in veils black as the blackened night, stark against the virgin white snow intrude, invade the silent winter city. No soothing lullaby, no hope of comforting warmth or shelter could take away the haunting chill of the sensation accompanied by this frightening vision. Writhing, wretched turning, howling; the sensation of sober, stinging, unrelenting, unforgiving hunger jolted the silent sleeper; penetrated and pierced the burrows of the earth's slumbering beasts. They brought the dreamer back, reminded him of the carnal necessity of his existence that thwarts one to hunt, to scurry like the hungry animal for meager morsels of flesh-fulfilling necessity.

Lucas awoke, continued along his way, allowed himself to be drawn, to be led by the natural compass of the Sun, whose divine mission it is to guide our soul. And she moved him, guided him, led him to an enormous, majestic, withered stone sundial in the midst of a luscious garden of yellow dandelions, uncultivated and overgrown. Embedded in this massive stone contraption adorned in intricate geometrical designs and a sharp sword like style that cast a long thin shadow on precisely the point marking the eighteenth hour read the cryptic letters: "[…] until the end of all time." He was fantastically dumbfounded by the precision of this parochial and sacred object that told of the commanding power of transitory time, governed by the ancient gods, regulated by the astrological constellations, the poles of west, east, north and south, and the significant shifts of Earth, Sun and Moon, – nature's natural clock. He pondered the tremendous foresight that must have been possessed by those who had erected such a monument in the name of time in long, long days of old and remembered that the very same Sun that illuminated this spectacular device was the same that now shone her eternal light on him. He saw in the thin shadow reflected from the long, sharp, sword-like style onto the stone obelisk, the fates of its maker reflected, gazing back at him; it became at once a medium connecting the great disparity between him and those who had lived in the time of its construction. What genius of the mind that enabled man to conceive of, yes, to uncover the mathematical formulas and equations, the riddles that lie behind the finite forms of our galaxy. He imagined that they must have been imprinted in him since the beginning of time and would be made known to him by means of the evolutionary process of deduction and recollection of the hidden secrets and powers locked inside the depthless expanses of the human mind.

He missed now the safe confines of home, felt a sweet longing for the consoling comfort of his bed, of his sweet abode, to escape his present state and to flee into the soothing comfort of soft, heavy sheets. He remembered many a night of sneaking under the bed covers, – and the pocket light with which he skimmed the pages of dictionaries, encyclopedias, old maps and books, – the symbolic candle he held up to the daily ritual that signified the end of a day's journey of careless, blissful and idol wonder and play, knowing all the while that the sweet luxury of sleep was just a light switch away. Sleep was not just the revitalization of flesh; it was something far more meaningful to him in that it marked the border between the previous day and the ushering in of a new day. How effortlessly we forget the pains and pleasures of the previous day when revitalizing sleep restores us. The fresh, budding morning of a brand new day signified boundless possibility and rebirth; opened up countless wonders yet untainted by the endless obstacles that awaited. Dreams of the most varied kind brushed the unconscious mind of this particular boy each night as he slipped into deep sleep. Fascinating the state in which we find ourselves once we have lost all power of our faculties of consciousness. Dreams take over and dominate the sedated mind; tiny disassociated fragments of our memories come to life and assemble themselves into series of the most unlikely of symbols. Inexplicable the elaborate configuration and sequence of images that we in our waking state could only scarcely conceive or reproduce, images over which we have no conscious mental control. What complex wonders of the mind must be at work to allow for such a process! The mind can conceive of an infinite number of things indeed! It can conjure schemes that far exceed that which is known or physically palpable to man. One can find the strangest illogicalness in the most logical of things and strange logic in the most illogical. Imagination, dreams, hope, – call it what you will; they comprise a faculty infinitely more powerful than that constituted by any of the physical senses. And the ability to conceive of the potentiality of that to which we have no logical reference serves as the driving force of human life, of our spiritual survival.

The boundless hours of illuminating light passed in the flickering moment of the now as the Sun had almost fully descended behind and beyond the wide and all-enveloping horizon. Follow the Sun! it proclaimed. Strands of thin, cottony clouds sailed slowly by under the violet sky and blended splendidly with the golden-brown, red, green and atomic-tangerine of Earth and our atmosphere, crowned and reflected by the fluorescent light of aurora borealis, – fuchsia, blue and green; became a rich palette, a perfect tapestry before which Lucas could observe and behold the complex dance in which these wonderful unearthly beings engaged. Combing and brushing the land with surgical care, they moved, no, they flowed toward a common destination, seemed to be following the fleeting light of the rapidly setting Sun. Lucas remembered once more; heard the overbearing ticks and tocks of the big grandfather clock in Mr. Woodcroft's abode. The sense of fleeting urgency tugged at his soul and he was filled with the enervating feeling that time was quickly running out. His ever so recent state of peaceful revelry was transformed now into panic and anxiety as he remembered that the Sun, which leads us naturally down the path of reflection and insight, would soon too disappear.

Now so infinitely far from home, his return to the irrecoverable world of comforting familiarity seemed impossible. He had the dream he had had on many an occasion in which he was flying lonesome in the nebulous depths of infinite space, searching for a new place, a new home. Halting suddenly in the midst of supersonic flight, he was now, as he had always been, brushed by that familiar panic that penetrated the nervy flesh through to the innermost depths of his soul, the fear that he had reached an irreconcilable point, in time, too infinitely and irreconcilably far removed from home to ever be able to return, and ahead, beyond, an endless black hole of distance and time separating him from the unknown. Imagine, just imagine the fear of such a prospect, of coming face to face with the abyss, the empty and inarticulate nothing that lie far beyond the limits of man's consideration; it would cause any man to come to the realization that there is no greater solace than in tangible, finite spaces.

The long forgotten memory of home, the safety of warm, heavy sheets and busy streets and of all that had brought him here simply dissipated in the vaporous clouds of time and space, seemed now like a distant dream. He became startlingly aware of his dilemma. He struggled vexingly with the prospect of staying in the old world or entering into the new one. Entering into the new world meant relinquishing all memory, both positive and negative, of his past. From the perspective of the celestial beings, history was negative memory and would only serve as an obstruction to man's further spiritual evolution, to the fulfillment of a new era, the new world they had in their design. It had shown itself to be destructive, as man had failed to learn from the mistakes of history.

And so, the slate would, in other words, be erased clean, and along with it, all the bad memories that plagued him throughout his entire life. At the same time, they were what made him the exceptional person he had become; they bred in him the most valuable quality of all: compassion. There was no refuting or rationalizing the recent events or the reasoning of the celestial beings. Their will was absolute, governed foremost by pure and perfect reason and logic, – a point in which they diverged most markedly from the human race, which was still predominantly governed by primitive passion; and evolution unhindered, unrestrained, was passion contained; intellect and reason balanced. Lucas was left to struggle with the decision of whether to enter into life in the new system or to forfeit the divine duty prescribed him, but with memories of his life and all previous experience in tact. The latter would, of course, have implied the plausibility of an afterlife or of some form or state of being in which memories of his life up to the present point would stay in tact. He was so sad, so terribly sad about it all, for everything that brought him here, life was still so precious, life was still so dear.

And so, the main philosophical

dilemma for Lucas lie in the choice of either appropriating the altruistic and selfless duty of mentor to a new generation of younglings toward the fulfillment of an ultimately pure and positive objective or forfeiting it in the favor of preserving his vital memories. The latter was a somewhat selfish choice, as it would, in Lucas' eyes, have served only toward the redemption of himself and himself alone, at the expense of the greater cause and the fulfillment of a higher calling. But how could they expect of him that he leave the only life he had ever known, a life to which he had throughout the span of his entire existence clung with every fleshy fiber of his being? Even if he were to have erased every last single, minute memory that bound him to it, he feared that he, within the deepest depths of his soul, would fight it to the very end. From whichever angle he viewed it, he couldn't, simply couldn't go back; couldn't erase that which he with every waking and dreaming step had come to know; couldn't undo every single sliver of fantastic debris that had etched itself into the very heart of him. Some might have seen this as a justification of a decision he had already long ago conceived. How exciting, how exhilarating the wonderful duplicity of it all!

And so, he was thrust into the decision to stay and to face the great unknown or to go back and forfeit all memory of his past. With both, there was, at least in his eyes and from his point of reasoning, no return. The first meant living on by abandoning all that came before, the second, by perishing, but doing so with the experience of the previous world in tact, untainted by the unknown future. For Lucas, the decision was somewhat simpler, if not for the fact that he had always lived that way, lived on a bare whim, lived on the diminishing expense of a tiny hope or two, on the promise of a simple, insignificant ray of light; left the winds of fate to sway him which and every way they may. And what dying despair did he feel when that light never came. It was always all or nothing with him, no in between. He took the unforgiving inequity of life and twisted it to suit his means, was dead set determined to approach life with the same merciless arbitrariness that it had shown him. He felt life, felt it with clenched tooth and to the very core of his fleshy nerve. The repercussions of his resolve had always been of little consequence to him. He felt for a moment now even a brush of pride and strength of will for his ability to effortlessly relinquish and abolish the past

124

and a world that showed him no mercy.

He lingered still for a brief moment, his left hand firmly grasping the stem of a dandelion; and he knew, knew that it was for the ambassador's sake and his sake alone that he felt a deep remorse, because embracing a new world meant living it without the memory of him. The four years that he had spent in his presence had become his lifetime, and the years that had preceded paled in significance, for what could have more bearing on a life; a lost and solitary soul than that which was so recent, so fresh in the mind, to experience, to emotion. He saw a dome-shaped construction in the far distance, fortified by light force, the lustrous, silvery white surface of which the light of the evening Sun so brilliantly illuminated. From silver flairs in the distance ignited flew thick blue, blush and bittersweet pink colored clouds that filled the atmosphere and rose to the sky up high, catching the eyes of the insignificant figures that stood on the other side of the recesses of jungle and marshes. This message was received by the distant onlookers, whose shouts of affirmation of his existence echoed through the green sea of bushes and trees. He made out from these figures, the forms of children moving, pulled by some drawing force upwards along the gradual incline that led to one of the fortresses that the creatures had erected. He watched as the number of the figures became increasingly sparser, until one by one, they were gone. When the dust of the colored clouds had finally faded, a perfect picture, a blended composition of sky and earth stood in perfect and serene silence and stillness. Not even the slightest wind whispered. A wonderfully and delightfully comforting, tepid and tranquil temperature governed the atmosphere. And he stood there with nothing but his lonely thoughts.

Eighth Chapter

And, so, Lucas found himself once more in that place from which he had this morning in heavy grief departed. Silence prevailed from within the inner confines of the quarters of the old wise man, the doctor of philosophy, the professor emeritus, the ambassador. This was strange and unaccustomed indeed, for he had seldom left his abode, had been confined by his ripe years to this cluttered, dingy and dusty but charming space that much resembled an antique book shop, with its stale, dusty, yet comfortingly warm earth-tone-hued décor, – and shelves upon shelves of ancient words that told of the painstaking plots and idle ideologies of men. The atmosphere, quite like its former occupant, boasted an exalting eccentricity and an air of strange familiarity, mixed with an all-absorbing and life-expending abyss of words. And alienating, – alienating because of the seeming intangibility of the ideas and ideals that they professed, for an eternity of human history had revealed their fallacy, saw millennia of countless fates unraveled and histories told, a world of facts, figures, myths and distress put to rest, swept away in the face of the forever fading now and never of this all-evading moment, this all too surreal circumstance in which he now found himself. In the corner of the room stood a glorious grandfather clock that tiredly and drudgingly, but determinedly and faithfully ticked and tocked and chronicled the fleeting passage of time, the aging of words. Its lustrous, golden pendulum blazed in sublime brilliance in the light shining through the aperture of the window, which, once penetrating the realm of the thick, dusty glass, dispersed a rainbow of reflections, exposed a kaleidoscope of colors, a prism of thin, translucent rays of fine, sparkling dust particles. They floated carelessly, danced with the light then froze in the sun-soaked space, giving it an almost decreased propensity, which only contributed to the vision of familiar and lulling antiquity in this otherwise drab space. Delicate, gray-white dust covered the old books like fresh fallen snow and glowed in the crisp incandescent light of the evening Sun. And basking in its warmth, Lucas mourned the dawn of the day, thought, noticed, remembered that the morning light quite differs from that of any other point of the eternal day, that it warms and delights more deeply, infuses the soul with vital energy, and instills in the mind, yes, the soul, a feeling, a lingering resonance of reverence, peace, insight and creative inspiration. And light through a window warms doubly, more intensely. And how he wished that this moment, this sensation would never dwindle.

The professor's absence seemed now, however, peculiarly irrelevant as Lucas chose instead, no, was somehow pulled by some summoning inclination to forget, to revel in the present picture of sensual and spiritual delight that the mixture of the special light of dusk with the color scheme of pastel blues, browns and yellows of the antiquated books produced, as if there was some message of grave significance to be inferred from it. He remembered in the brief and fleeting bliss occasioned by this image the endless stories contained in some of these old books, which Mr. Woodcroft had on quite many an occasion recited to him, in an effort, as he called it, to further his erudition. They contained philosophizing philosophies, theorems, wonderful sagas and legends long gone. One had spoken of the complex relationship that exists, no, that must exist, between eternity and time, of their relation to us, and of our ability, our capacity, by means of the natural gift of our human faculties of intellect and reason, – or perhaps of a faculty borrowed from some infinitely more profound source, – to remember, in moments precisely such as this, those things that precede us. We feel such a mind and soul afflicting affinity to the things contained in such stories and in the pictures that they evoke, an inextricable connection to things that existed before us without ever having shared any real physical connection to them; they revealed to us nonetheless that which is eternal, led us to higher contemplation of the abstract images of the infinite, of which all things manifest are a mere finite extension; they impressed in us a grain of that which was, is and forever will be throughout the endless years. Every sentence, every word contained within it a glimpse, a mere fractional fragment of the spherical whole, showed us in cumulative fragments, reflections of the entirety of not only human history, but of all that which held it. The words were, after all, a simple means, the telling itself, however, the catalyst of lofty progress. And what was history without the human hand to write it, the human mind to conceive it, human words to express it? Was it the image created by the illuminating rays of the Sun on the withered, pale brown, maroon and blue dusty book covers that inspired such thoughts? Or were they thoughts that had forever resided in the unfathomable depths of the mind before man's existence, imbued in him by the supreme source that preceded?

Lucas lost himself for a moment in the mysticism emanating from this ever so delectable and sensually scrumptious scene and remembered once more his current state. At once serene and strangely stimulating, having forgotten it in the surreal occurrences of the eternal day in Sun's splendor, he remembered once more his grief. As heart-wrenching as it was to bear, it was something comfortingly and soothingly familiar nonetheless. He hoped with all his might to retrieve, to recall, to remember if even a fragment of the memories that had here once flourished. But nothing of the kind remained in this now abandoned space but a few small keepsakes: a silver drinking flask, an antique, hand-crafted wooden jewelry box, a pair of gold white porcelain-encrusted binoculars and, on a towering stack of periodicals, the professor's thick spectacles. A mournful melancholy overcame him anew as he remembered once more the grief of the morning light. A remorseful nostalgia and the prospect of parting with the familiar objects and remnants of yesterday's world flooded his heart like crashing waters. Then came a sudden sorrow, a grave affliction of the soul for the sake of the realization that it was not so much the objects themselves, but rather the sake of the inextricable memories and experiences so significantly woven through them that would make parting from them so difficult, so impossible. He mourned not only them, but also that which they represented, for they were the reflection, the chronicles of countless years of human progress. In them, he saw the only means through which to stamp into the wretched, cursed and careless world his maddened fury. To see them now stripped of any and all the significance and meaning that he and the weary world had only yesterday so ardently, so unavowingly, so uncontemplatingly attached to them elicited a tear in his mind's eye. Countless ages from now, the countless pages upon pages onto which countless words upon words are inscribed will long have perished. But the ideas that inspired them are of an essence far-exceeding and forever enduring. He felt in the abyss that awaited, a negation of all his life's memories. He stood a short while, a brief eternity,

132

mourning the departure of this legacy, of Mr. Woodcroft and of all the authors of the very books on these shelves that contained the aging words conceived on the fragile foundation of something so small, so simple as an idea, now but a mere dwindling afterthought of what was. He mourned unrequited love, unconsummated hope and unfulfilled fate; found it impossible to come to terms with the notion that it was all too late. He wanted to be loved, loved unconditionally and without contingency, to have been loved in the time before the fall; to have been loved by those who had always and forever faltered in their love, who had failed to show him the love that he sought, to nourish him with the love that he needed.

Oh the sweet accounts of careless, unrepentant youth! He remembered the countless visits that he used to make with his mother to the aunt with the golden hair and golden teeth. He took pleasure in taking in the sedating scent of cigarettes, found strange novelty and delightful distraction in the sight of translucent, silky strands of gray-white smoke as they hovered then merged into a soft, misty and murky cloud of vapor, conjured fascinating forms, sat and stood still, static in the conditioned air. The gold-tainted walls and rugs bore witness to copper pennies, silver nickels, dimes and nursery rhymes; fortunes in coffee stains and small coffee cups; stolen sips and chocolate chips; the pungent, sweet aroma of coffee beans and the rhythmic tinkering of sewing machines. What infinitely simple things can capture the imagining soul of a bright and striving youth in the suckling years before the worries and scurries of school, of life set in! But, in this finite world, we never quite become accustomed to the fact that all good things must inevitably come to an end, a reality that pained him, the chosen one, the lonely, pale-blue-eyed daydreamer especially. For him, every single goodbye meant bitter end, mournful repose, – and always the end.

He stared with unquenchable idealism and hope into the framed pictures that hung inanimately on the wall and on old antique dressers, images that eternalized and sang of a moment once frozen in time. They moved him, but even more, they pained and alienated, because they were a moment once enjoyed, but that remained forever elusive, – a reminder of what we once were but have ceased to be. They leave us burning in longing for the moment captured within the image of unfulfilled ideals and dreams.

Powerless, we gaze into the trembling, frozen image with our eyes and wish to release it from its static sphere, from that finite moment in the all-evading finitude of our experience. He always found it painful to ruminate on old photos and at once a tormenting wish to immerse himself in the moment of someone he once was physically, yet to whom he found himself now infinitely detached, and the moment that was once immediate experience of that which itself at one point as presence revealed, constantly evades us, yes, flies away forever. Irreconcilable reality! Haunting memories are all we have, – ghosts without aim or vision. He was haunted by the shadows of his past, which made living in the moment and for the moment so abysmally painful. Photos are remnants and rubble of the ruins of our past, a shallow symbol of dreams, hopes and ideals, without soul, without essence. A constant battle is waged between the image and the memory of that which the image represents, of which we are the unfortunate casualties. He tried to capture one last, final glimpse, just one more of the moments trapped, static in framed, dusty pictures.

He opened the wide, majestic bay windows in the corner of the pentagon shaped study where he had, on so many a night, – too many to count –, during the late hours after the ambassador had retired into his sleeping quarters, spent restless nights writing, wondering, hoping, dreaming. When it all came down to it, he couldn't, simply couldn't reconcile past and present. Precious memories of his past festered in the deepest, innermost glowing depths of his fragile soul; rooted out every seed that good will and pleasure nourished. He had long lost touch with that essence, that instinct in man that makes him linger for still a while and seek hope and new potential in the light of a new day. He saw no more hope in light, believed no longer in the good in man. Late! It was all too late! No promise of the new system could recover that which had forever been lost. A gentle force from the summer breeze filled the room from without, expunged the stale air of old and consumed it with the new breath of fresh and vital hope. Deprived, depleted, impoverished, he breathed it in, inhaled it with insatiable zeal. And here, he beheld the most majestic of all visions. The supreme light of the majestic Sun amplified in supernova, almost blinded the eye, ruptured the soul. Paralyzed, impotent and powerless in the tempestuous power of the infinitely greater and greater growing light, he was drawn helplessly to the magnifying pull of the Sun. Perfect euphoria infused the senses. Tangible objects; buildings, houses, parochial forms of old disembodied, dematerialized, dispersed and dissolved atom by atom, particle by particle into a neon nebula, a vacuous cloud of fine silky sand particles, danced in the glow of the neon white and yellow night, until, finally, they were gone. Luscious tears poured from his soul as he held the professor's spectacles close to his chest, shed a tear or two now and dawned a humble, solemn smile in affirmation of the beautiful moment and in acceptance of his fate. Millions of secrets locked inside his mind revealed themselves to him in the instance of this infinite and all-encompassing moment. And there, from the blended composition of the elemental light emerged the second Sun. The horizon disappeared as Sun, sky and Earth fused now into a symphony of euphoric sound, light and vision. And then, from every point of the blurred horizon, from east and west, north and south, from below and above, from within and without the inner spheres and outer spaces, the creatures from sky descended approached in perfectly planned precision, engaged in a methodical march of mathematical movements, – a calculated and choreographed dance of mindful intent to carry out their divine device.

The rebuilding began. Unshaped and unarticulated matter materialized and concretized as if out of thin air into visually and tangibly conceivable shapes and forms. He saw it happen, witnessed, gaping in gasping amazement, each atom from the flattened ruins of the finite forms of yesterday's world reconvene in shapes and forms unfathomed. Their formation mimicked the composition of celestial spheres as they, slowly and steady moving in well thought out lines like the stars and planets of our galaxy, a microcosm, microscopic mimicries of the macrocosmic spaces of our universe, presented themselves so sensationally in intricately plotted patterns visible and conceivable to the human mind, the existence of which had made themselves known to us in small, subtle signs and smithereens in the human mind upon our conception and evoked in us now a recollection of the incalculable patterns of the infinite. And after the long, elaborate procession of unearthly beings seemed to have reached its end; they stood, lingered as

138

if in a moment of mindful contemplation, meditation and appraisal of their work.

And, as it all drew to an end, as the light of life grew faint and into the eve of the endless night gently faded, Lucas could see how and where it had all gone amiss. He saw in scattered and fading fragments the symptoms that had led to the fall: the gross indifference, the disenchantment, the greed, the entitlement in extremity, the corruption of heart, and most apparent of all, the great disconnect. He looked up this one last and final time and surrendered himself now completely and emphatically to the vast and barren sky. Some might say that he perished in vain, that his passing was his ultimate defeat in the face of time. But to him, it was his one, last crying roar against the arbitrary inequity of it all, of life, of time, of the wretched human experience.

"Now you're really getting deep."

"What can I do? It just goes on; it never stops."

"I know. It's not easy. It wasn't supposed to be this way. It was all supposed to be so simple."

"I don't suppose that even you can help me now. I don't think that there is any help for me really. Is there any point to this?"

"Is there any point to anything really?"

"I was once so young, so full of life."

"You're not alone."

"But they're just words."

"They're what you feel. Do you think that what they say is any more important? They're just like you. We're all the same really. In the end, it won't have mattered much anyway. Care to join me?"

"I'd rather not. It's safer here. Besides, it's cold outside."

"You worry too much."

"I'm always worried. That's why I need you now more than ever. You can't go. What will happen to me, to them if you go?"

"They don't have any need for me, anyway. They haven't for a long time. It's all right though. I can't say I didn't see it coming. It will soon all be over, anyway. It's time, a better time than any I suppose."

"Should I take a souvenir or two?"

"There won't be any need for that where we're going."

Who could have dreamt, who would have thought in their wildest dreams the affliction and destruction of thousands of years and the billions of fates that endured in endless screams the suffering and sickness that plagued us so? Only written words will bear the mark of the history of time, and endless time the stamp of finite words that into eternal thoughts transmuted, of the flickering moment of this transient life, of the trifling trivialities, – those miniscule matters that mattered so much; they will live on as delicate recollection in the human mind, awoken from time to time by a sweet melody or a gentle summer breeze. Unfathomable was the technology and ingenuity of the beasts that showed us the way to the light again, a mere fraction of the power of which they would come to bestow upon the chosen ones of us. And with time, the secrets of these wise and sentient ones would be made known to us. And it was proclaimed that this wonderful gift would henceforth be utilized and implemented toward the means and only that means for which it had been intended, namely, for the betterment and prosperity of all living things on this planet.

A sea of bright, young faces assembled in one of the colossal fortresses that they had of earth and light forged; it, and the many that they had far and everywhere throughout erected, would serve as centers, – the nuclei, or brain, of the new system, without from which the exchange of knowledge, thoughts and ideas would freely flow. The younglings looked up collectively with attentive prudence and undisturbed silence at an overbearing form that stood now before them. That which they here from the sentient being received was a new manifesto of sorts, – nature's decree. It proclaimed that no profit of the sort that fueled human incentive in the days before the fall would henceforth be sought. Each and every single individual, equal in life, equal in love, will, through whatever power lie in his grasp and by virtue of any means in his capacity, strive to contribute to the good and preservation of the system. By seeing his most basic needs and interests met, so too would he be inclined toward the fulfillment of the interests of all wonderful human beings on this planet. May the prosperity, – physical and spiritual –, of every human being attest to the flawlessness of a system that suppresses no one, exploits no one, neglects no one. And so it was decreed that the love that here takes root is born of soul's pure intention; connections are henceforth made and bound by love. With the absence of those gadgets that humans divided and from the light of the supreme source distracted held, they would once again find their way back to one another, to nature. The contributions of those who had long ago perished, those who had harbored a spark of the bright light in their hearts would not be for naught. Their spirit, their name would live on and throughout the generations to come. But, as concerns the others, the creatures saw it pertinent that they be stricken from this planet, their doings undone and the memory of them rendered obsolete. Some higher reasoning of the beasts beyond that which is in our human capacity to comprehend dictated that this be so. Perhaps it would some day be revealed to those in whose hands the light of the new system had been kindled. Call it arbitrary. But was there not one action by the hand of man since the conception of the age of the moving machines that had not proved itself to be grossly absolute, hideously arbitrary? The elders had been too far removed from the light of the stars, buried too great the burden of the former world. They were irreparable rubble and remnants of the old world. Their removal, so the creatures, would ensure the seamless and unhindered propagation of the new system that they had in their design.

No tribunal, no trial, but the one true and divine justice were here and henceforth to be exacted by decree of the universal law, – law of the heavens, a law governed by true impartiality, reason and logic, – a far cry from that hypocritical and inherently partial, flawed and corrupt law that governed human beings in the times before the fall, in a system that saw human exploit, oppression and suffering legitimized, systematized, institutionalized. The creature conjured now an image, or something of the like, of that inanimate artifact, that symbol of the human monetary system that had bound us, now become the symbol of a terribly erroneous time, of a passing paradigm. He held it up for all to see, burned into our memory, the erring ways of history.

It was a shame, it was a mess, but still it happened nonetheless. There's nothing more that we can do than start afresh, yes, start anew. Those technologies of old served that capital flow, but if they serve their purpose right, they could help the seed of mankind grow. We're only in the initial stage of a story in its infancy. With the knowledge we have gained today, we can make the transformation real; it can be conceived, and so, alas, it too can be real.

22155752R00083